The Lolita Man

Bill James

The Lolita Man

A Foul Play Press Book

W. W. Norton & Company
New York • London

Copyright © 1986 by Bill James
First American edition published 1991 by Foul Play Press,
a division of W. W. Norton & Company, New York
First published as a Foul Play Press paperback 1998

Library of Congress Cataloging-in-Publication Data

James, Bill
The Lolita man : a detective Colin Harpur novel / Bill James.
p. cm.   ISBN 0-88150-198-0
I. Title
PR6060.A44L65   1991
823'.914—dc20   90-27391
                                 CIP

Printed in the United States of America

ISBN 0-393-31782-X pbk.

W. W. Norton & Company, Inc.
500 Fifth Avenue, New York, NY 10110
http://www.wwnorton.com

W. W. Norton & Company Ltd.
10 Coptic Street, London WC1A 1PU

1 2 3 4 5 6 7 8 9 0

The Lolita Man

I

Ruth Avery used to say that making love with Harpur was like being in bed with all of E-Division. He would hang his handset radio on a coat hook and the chatter and orders bubbled away while they talked over it or held each other or lay thinking about the need to get up soon or about the future, if they had one together. Names they both knew gave company through the static to their best minutes, and their best minutes were as good as Harpur had forecast to himself when Ruth was still someone out of reach, just the well-fleshed wife of an underling.

Occasionally his own name would come up and he would have to answer. Sometimes it would happen at exactly the wrong moment, kicking dead all the magic for that day. No lasting damage seemed done, though. She understood police life and knew it did not stop because two people were having a sweet time. They would get a laugh out of it and plan for the next week.

Afternoons suited her best, when her children were at school. She would not let him come to her house and they could not go to his so they used one of a handful of third-rate hotels in rotation. No need for five stars when it was only a couple of hours, all in bed. Once when she was depressed or angry she had called it a screwing arrangement.

He would pay for the room in advance so they could slip away in the late afternoon without explaining why. These hotels were on to a fine thing: just a couple of sheets for the laundry and no call on their Shredded Wheat. In France, apparently, you could take a room by the hour for love, but not here. They had considered asking their Euro MP to demand uniformity.

Today, his radio had been beautifully unintrusive, the message all small stuff, none of it on his plate. Now, it was coming up to four o'clock and they would have to get dressed soon so Ruth could shop for the tea before going home.

'What do they think you do these afternoons?' she asked.

'Just dropping out of view for hours. Nobody ever asks questions? Someone of your rank carrying a handset when there's no operation – that's not normal, surely?'

'I have to. I use an ancient car – better cover but no radio in it.'

Who knew what they thought? They were police, so they probably thought the worst and had it right. What they thought did not matter unless it reached the ultimate brass, and that hadn't happened yet. As far as he knew it hadn't.

'This is love talk?' he protested, drawing her to him.

'That's what I like with you, you do talk about it.'

'Half the joy.'

'No, not as much as half.'

'No, maybe not.'

She moved her legs for him. 'Oh, no, nothing like half,' she muttered, and then for a while they did not talk and it seemed no loss at all.

The radio did, though, and spoke his name. For these summit seconds he gave it the big ignoral. Her legs and arms had tightened on him and their mouths held each other's. For all the nick knew he could be deep into some tricky bit of surveillance, his radio switched off for silence.

'What would I do without you?' he said, not to the radio.

'Give better attention to your career?'

He climbed out of bed and answered. Could he look at an incident at the King Richard Hotel, the girl asked.

'What's the nature?'

'To be notified by the officer already present, sir.'

Ruth was dressing swiftly on the other side of the bed.

'It's A priority, sir.'

That was some new jargon Iles had introduced as soon as he moved in as number two, meaning drop everything and get there. Harpur, too, began to dress. If they feared putting details over the air it was something dark.

Seated on a pink wooden chair in her jeans and jumper, Ruth laced up a pair of training shoes. 'What a great life you have, don't you, Colin?' she said, grinning. 'First some love, then, right on cue, a helping of urgent work, something to make you feel needed again.'

And she meant it. There was no sarcasm.

'I'd rather we could stay,' he replied.

She looked disbelieving. From the first time he had spoken to her months ago, when she was a wife not a widow, he had seen she was very bright. They kissed and went out separately into the struggling sunshine of an English March. Always when he left her after these meetings he feared it could be the last, dreaded that she might lose patience with the scruffy rooms, the secretiveness, the hurry, the fact that he always went home to Megan. Each time Ruth turned up was a bonus.

Less than half an hour later he was in another hotel bedroom, a more chic sort of place altogether: thick, warm carpet, television, green tiled bathroom *en suite*. Nice coloured prints of historical battles decorated the walls, as part of the King Richard theme. Long lace curtains fluttered in a small early Spring breeze through the half-open window.

Perhaps, at just the time he had been with Ruth on the other side of the town, this room, too, had been secretly in use. A mousy-haired girl of about thirteen lay unclothed on top of the bed's turquoise coverlet, her eyes closed as if in sleep, but not in sleep. Her face and neck were deeply scratched and bruised and the angle of her head on the brilliant white pillow seemed all wrong. One of her baby breasts had been torn as if by teeth and there was blood on the coverlet under her haunches. Harpur paused just inside the door. A middle-aged man was unrolling a plastic walk-way across the carpet and Harpur waited until he had finished.

'We can't cover her until pix, sir.'

'Has he broken her neck?'

'We think so. The doc's coming.' Hubert Scott, long-time a detective sergeant, must have seen these things before, but looked dazed by grief or anger or both and his voice for the moment had grown high and tense. 'I gather the Assistant Chief is on his way. He was on the other side of the patch when the first call came.'

'What have we got?'

'Little, so far. A dozen men looking. Road blocks. We're finding out what we can from staff and other guests.'

'He actually brought her here, booked in? Reception saw him, then?' It was beyond belief. Even in the presence of the body he felt almost elated. This could be the first description they'd ever had. Christ, the Lolita Man had started acting like that first Lolita man in the book, visiting hotels with his little bird. This little bird was called Fiona.

'That's not how it was,' Scott replied.

Yes, beyond belief.

'The girl and her parents are guests here, sir. They're out for the afternoon at a golf do. The girl stayed alone. It's a motel, the biggest in this part of England, guests buzzing about all the time, coming and going, even in March. There are chalets and bungalows as well as this main building. Nobody knows anybody. Entry's a doddle, and escape.'

'So it could all have been over in half an hour?'

'Easily. It's not like the others. Then he held the girls, what, two days, three? Might not even be the same bloke.'

'Jesus, don't say that. Yes, it has to be the same – age of the kid, method of killing, the kind of rape. We'll hear if this one was incompetent, too. But we can vary how he works. We thought we knew him properly. We don't.'

The photo crew arrived and Scott busied himself keeping them on the plastic so they would disturb no soil fragments left on the carpet.

'Who found her?' Harpur asked. 'Did the parents come back?'

'They don't know yet. We're looking for them.'

'God.'

'A maid brought Fiona's tea just before 4 p.m. The parents had left instructions. It's here.' A tray with a slopped glass of Coca Cola and an éclair on it stood on a small table. The maid had done damn well not to spill more when she opened the door on this.

'Vehicle?'

'We haven't identified that, though we're working on it, of course.'

'So, what instructions to the road blocks?'

Scott nodded, admitting the hopelessness of it. 'Just general, sir. They're to look for anything out of the ordinary. He could be marked about the face.'

Harpur examined her nails for hair or skin. The hands were still warm.

Iles entered very softly. 'A bit out of the pattern, Colin?'

'In some respects, sir. Yes, it's a shock.'

'But we'll have the bastard this time, for sure. Good God, he's put himself on show. This is not some bloody back lane or field, like the others. It's a major English hotel.'

'That's what I thought, sir.'

'There you are then, it must be right. March has always been my lucky month.' The Assistant Chief stood over the child. 'Poor, poor wee one. She would never have been a beauty, but what does that matter? Such a risk, to have a girl child. Always has been. Think of Eva Braun. Nothing's going to change it and not us for certain, even if we are computerised.' He bent down towards her, almost touched her scored cheek with his own. 'Never mind, Fiona, it's past now.' He straightened. 'This makes five.'

'Three on our ground, sir, two on theirs. We're virtually at the boundary of our patch here. The King Richard is just inside.'

Iles's voice changed to a low snarl, meant only for Harpur. 'That great gulf between them and us. When we have this character we'll do it on our own, Col – make those sods over in the county look the thicks they are. Yes, this – this bugger is ours. Look, Col, we'll pick up a stack of leads but we give nothing to those county twats. Well, of course not. This guy is unique, isn't he? All the sexologists tell us rapists hardly ever kill. Oh, I know there's the Boston Strangler and that joker who got among the Chicago nurses, but it's rare and especially in rapists of kids. We'll be in the textbooks. So why should we let them in from the county? Would they put anything our way?' His voice had come back to normal volume.

The photographer finished at the bed and Iles helped Hubert Scott reverently cover the body. 'I ask you, would they put anything our way, Col?'

'Possibly nothing beyond the basics, sir.'

'What do you think, Hubert?'

'They'd give us nothing, sir.'

'You're dead right. I like someone who says clearly what he means.'

Harpur prowled the room.

'Desire, what a dynamo, though, Col,' Iles said. 'Think how much simpler and calmer it would make everything if jerking off was really all it's cracked up to be by the theorists. Get all that pushy semen safe into hankies. Now, I lay me. Instead, this. All those future years of hair lacquer and telly viewing obliterated.'

Someone from the hotel brought a dustpan and brush and Scott started gathering fragments of mud from the carpet. They might come from the Lolita Man and they might tell a tale. Iles watched approvingly. These two were very close, and Harpur had an idea they belonged to the same Lodge. Scott was something big and colourful in the Brotherhood, now and then getting his name in the *Daily Telegraph*.

'Only child?' Iles asked.

'I don't think we know,' Scott replied. 'She was the only one staying with them.'

'God, I hope she's not,' Iles said. 'Who's informing the parents? Please tell me it's not some heavy, stinking of Jack Daniels.'

'One of the girls, sir,' Scott replied.

'Fine. I'll see them myself as soon as they arrive and try to talk them out of looking at the body yet. A memory like that could stick for ever, wreck a mind. Tell me I can promise them we'll nail him, Col.'

'Of course, sir.'

'Thank you, thank you. This is so much the worst part of our job, isn't it – to witness the misery of parents? The slightest comfort one can offer is worthwhile, and occasionally the assurance of retribution can help. And, Col, when you say we can do it, we can do it, can't we, without the least aid from that Mick-led troupe in the county?' He was whispering again.

'Do you think that might be important to the parents, sir? Won't they simply want this man caught, no matter how?'

Iles went back to the bed and with immense gentleness uncovered Fiona's face again, as if to read her own wishes there. 'You might have something, Col, I must admit. But let me put it this way for you, shall I? There is, after all, a balanced way of looking at all these problems.' He paused to choose his words. Several times Harpur had heard Iles say he prized reason and careful argument. 'Simply, Col, I won't have that glib band from next door getting in on any of the good stuff we unearth, is that clear? We ask that swarm for nothing, we give them nothing. As a matter of fact, I'm thinking of proposing that as the new motto of the Force – ditch all the Latin crap about *fidelitas*. Bloody profs call their dogs that.'

'The point is, sir, they might already have a lot on this man from their own incidents. It could speed things and speed is important. We might lose more kids.'

'We take nothing from them. The child herself wouldn't wish it, I sense that. We'll have all this sewn up by Easter – in fact by the end of March. The Chief will want it finished before he retires.'

A woman sergeant approached and said the parents had arrived. 'They would like to see their daughter, sir. They've been told the whole thing.'

Iles replaced the cover with the same tenderness as before. 'Take me down to them, sergeant, would you please? They must do whatever they wish, of course, but let me talk to them first. I'll tell them that Fiona deserves nothing but the best this Force can offer, and it will be forthcoming.'

2

11 June
I bought this lovely diary with green leather covers yesterday with money I had from mummy and daddy for my fourteenth birthday, which was on 9 June, a quite important birthday for a girl. It will be a very, very secret diary, not humorous like Adrian Mole but to do with life.

This book must know first there is a wonderful he in my life. The wonderful he has been in my life for four days, since 7 June, I shall never forget that date. Wonderful 7 June. Today he was there again. He has dark, dark eyes that look at me. His car is a blue Lagonda with white wheels and leather straps around the bonnet, which is long. He sits at the wheel and watches me. The number plate is a special one, DE1. I do not yet know his name so I shall call him Mr Dark Eyes, which fits these letters and is also like his eyes.

I do not think he smokes. His hair is dark and not too long but long enough and his sun tan is deep but not from a lamp. I think he has been abroad, such as Morocco or Naples or some other city, not on a Thomson but carrying out some particular vital mission or looking after various properties of his. The window of his motor is open and he lets his arm lie outside with no rings on his hand. I see him in different places, always in his blue Lagonda with some of his dark hair hanging over his forehead. I am so pleased if he does not smoke, owing to lung cancer and people's breath.

14 June

He, my wonderful he, or Dark Eyes as I call him, came again today. His car is changed. Now it is a blue Ferrari, ashine and full of power, I am sure, with its spare wheel strapped on the back. This one is DE2. Wonderful he was not changed, though. Still he watches me, his dark hair hanging over his forehead attractively. Our eyes meet in a silent contact. Always I make sure to be alone, hoping I shall see him, and I tell nobody about him, not so far. It is our wonderful secret. One day he will speak to me and I shall tell him that my name is Cheryl-Ann and also tell him that I admire Lagondas and Ferraris so much. Thereupon he will speak his own name and I will say, No, you are called Dark Eyes. He will smile and say, Very well, Cheryl-Ann. He has wonderful teeth, not too big. I hate those big ten-commandment teeth. Good night, wonderful Mr Dark Eyes. Remember 7 June is OUR wonderful day.

18 June

I do not know how tall wonderful he is for always he is seated at the wheel of his powerful motor. But I think he is tall, not too tall like a sick stick, but no high-rise shoes. It is a different car today, an Aston Martin of deepest blue and the registration is DE3. Personal numbers like these are extremely expensive so it is clear he is extremely rich. I think I like the Aston Martin best of all. I do not know why he has chosen me from among so many for there are lots of girls for him to look at. One day I shall be able to ask him why he chose me and he will say he is more myself than I am. He's always, always in my mind: not as a pleasure, any more than I am always a pleasure to myself, but as my own being.

No moustache or beard adorns his face and I'm sad about this for these adornments give a man a strong look sometimes, though not always. But wonderful he does not look weak, I don't mean that. Yet one day when we speak I shall mention to him a moustache and beard saying how they would go so well with his dark eyes. What does he like best about me? I have wondered a great deal about this. Is it my creamy skin or my hair, so yellow and fine? It is well known that opposite kinds of people attract each other, as in an extremely famous play by William Shakespeare called *Othello*, which ends in what is known as tragedy for the girl and everybody. The black man is tricked into killing her, it is not his real will, he loves her because she is so beautiful and fair. Her death brings what is known as catharsis but it is sad all the same.

Perhaps wonderful he also likes the very light blue colour of my eyes, I do not think he has ever seen my wonderful smile.

19 June

Joy lives in me and my heart flies. Once more today our eyes met in silent contact. It would be such a terrible day if he did not arrive. Today he was wearing his grey leather jacket, soft, thick leather, so expensive. Perhaps the jacket is a bomber, I cannot tell because he is seated in the blue Aston Martin. His shoulders in the jacket look so wide and strong and his arms seem very powerful. I think he must be on weights. Now I think that perhaps he does smoke, there is a stain on his fingers, and this is very sad indeed.

His shirt is silk, I think, with a nice small collar and I could see the edge of the sleeves of the shirt under the cuffs of his grey leather jacket. I like this effect. I think he knows about colours and what are the best colours together. It is not too shiny or new, the jacket. I hate new leather that shines, but it is not old or shabby either, he is too prosperous for that.

3

'My God,' Megan snarled quietly, 'it's time this annual farce was scrapped. All chums together – like hell.'

'It can be useful,' Harpur said.

'An imperial pain.'

He gazed around the large room. Perhaps his wife had it right: the smell of bogus comradeship could grow very ripe at these joint gatherings of the two Forces. But a midsummer day's cricket match and après-game party at the club had been in the calendar from before the Bow Street Runners, and now and then it might do a bit of good. Not oftener and not more, but that was something.

The Chief ended his little speech as this year's host. 'And although we may have expressed our traditional healthy rivalry through cricket today, I want to say now that the working harmony and cooperation between us and the county have never been greater, never more fruitful. I would like to offer a special word of thanks to my opposite number, Vince Ethan, and his admirable deputy, Mark Lane. Working together, as ever, we'll bring this terrible Lolita case to an end, I know it. We must. It will probably not surprise you to learn that, although I had intended to bring my retirement forward to next month I have decided, with Home Office accord, that I cannot go until we have cleared this matter. I would not be able to rest. When I leave this job I hope to pass on to my successor a healthy community, not one poisoned by a ghastly, perverse monster.'

Barton resumed his seat, smiling modestly through the cigar smoke, head back in a fine attempt at pride and resolution. He looked pretty bad, but there had been many times since the Lolita Man started when Harpur had seen him worse.

Vincent Ethan and Lane led the applause and Iles shouted a few 'Hear hears' and a 'Bravo'.

'I'd really like to go home now,' Megan said.

'We can't. Not yet. Please, love.'

People were leaving their tables and beginning to circulate. A woman Megan seemed to know pretty well began talking to her, thank God, and that crisis passed. Megan had never shown much patience with police politics.

On his way to congratulate Barton, Iles touched Harpur's sleeve. 'Have you had a good look at those two, Col?' he asked, pointing his thumb, low down, at Ethan and Lane. 'Talk about fucking crud. I've been fraternising.' He put his mouth close to Harpur's ear. 'Look, they're on to something big, I know the bastards are.'

'About the Lolita Man?'

'What else? They play baffled – of course they do, but I reckon they could pounce any day. It's in their damn voices. They're going to make a glorious, triumphant show out of this and leave us wiping shit off our faces.'

'Sometimes I feel I don't care who gets him, as long as he's out of the way. I don't want to see any more kids' corpses.'

Iles looked enraged but said: 'That's certainly a viable point of view, Col. You bring a fair and open mind to things – admirable. And such sensitivity. Would you consider thinking of it this way, though: if they do it, that bit of dandruff, Lane, could probably walk into Barton's job when he goes. Lane is i/c Operations over in the Papal State, my equivalent. All the credit would come to him. They'd canonise the sod. Our Police Authority has been pretty sensible on the whole but even they couldn't ignore that kind of achievement.'

'I'd heard he could be a contender.'

'Bully for you. We'd all heard, but he's talking as if the thing is cut and dried. So is Big Arse, his wife.'

'He might not be too bad.'

'Are you drunk or mad?' Iles replied. 'Ah, Mrs Harpur, how

radiant you look. These are banal occasions, yet you maintain a splendid cheerfulness and good humour.' He moved away.

Megan beckoned Harpur. 'Darling, I've something for your comfort. Sybil here was saying the girl murders seem to make absolutely no impact on the mind of her own fourteen-year-old daughter, or her friends.'

'Good. Our kids are the same.'

'You know Sybil, don't you? Sybil Day. Her husband's firm does the catering here – all your big functions.'

'Mr Barton always invites us. We have to taste the food first! It's true what Megan says. All my daughter is concerned about is, first, flash cars – always on to us to get a Lagonda or a Ferrari or an Aston, some hope – and, second, her school exams, *Othello, Wuthering Heights*, etcetera. I honestly believe that those steamy stories are more real to her than anything that happens around here. We get the quotes from breakfast to bedtime. It's giving me an education myself. How's this for a bit of Brontë?' She was a small, thin, even frail woman but made her voice large now as she switched to high passion. ' "He is more myself than I am. He's always, always in my mind, not as a pleasure, any more than I am always a pleasure to myself, but as my own being." '

'Top marks,' Harpur declared.

Ruth Avery was here tonight, looking great. Barton liked to do all he could to brighten her life since the torture and murder of her husband by a bank gang. That was a long time ago now, but the horror of it stayed fresh. Harpur knew nobody better than the Chief for human touches. His authentic soft centre was one reason these kid cases hit him so badly, and one reason he had grown weak: Iles, with all that uncanny vigour and cleverness, was getting beyond his control.

They were persuading Barton to the piano now, so he and his wife could do their yearly programme of Victorian songs. 'The Lambeth Walk', performed in gross, lampoon cockney, with everyone dancing and picking up the chorus, was always the climax. Barton hated London, especially its police, because of something far back in his career. Occasionally, Iles tried to unearth what it was, through friends in the Met.

Megan and Sybil edged away. 'We'll go and chat to Mrs Iles,' Megan said. 'She looks neglected, poor duck.'

Was it really such a good thing that Sybil Day's daughter and her friends showed no anxiety about the Lolita Man? Sometimes Harpur wished girls would worry more, and take more care. Obviously, nobody wanted these kids to become neurotic, scared of leaving the house. But the Lolita Man had been quiet for a long time now, and Harpur dreaded that he might make another move soon.

Iles was talking and laughing with Ethan and Lane and their wives. Christ, the ACC might have read things accurately: Ethan and Lane did look pleased with themselves, as if about to score. They might be sitting on something. Iles had exceptional antennae. At the moment, he seemed to be giving deep and respectful attention to Lane, who was apparently demonstrating a point about spin bowling. Iles had gone in at number six this afternoon and made seventy-eight not out, in his elegant and carefree way, beating them more or less on his own. His dinner jacket fitted to that neat, high-flier's physique like an envelope around a hearty cheque. In a while Iles put an arm on Lane's shoulder and the five of them made for the bar like long-time friends.

The singing boomed. To avoid it, Harpur crossed the room and went out on to the club terrace. It was eleven o'clock but still passably light and he made out the flags on top of the King Richard Hotel, and alongside it the gleam of motorway surface which could have carried the Lolita Man miles clear in either direction as soon as it was over with Fiona, the plain little kid, more than three months ago, in March. A dozen competing descriptions of what he might look like had come from the hotel and ten colours between black and yellow for his possible car, if he had one.

From where he stood now Harpur could gaze out over a wide slice of the town and surrounds. The Lolita Man could be down there, under his eyes, lying low, or maybe not lying low tonight. How would it be if they had a call and turned up in tuxedos and patent shoes and a bit more than half pissed? Would the parents of a dead and raped girl understand about the importance of the inter-Force cricket tourney? The Chief and Mrs

Barton had reached 'You Always Hurt The One You Love'.

The three months without an attack was the longest pause since the Lolita Man began. Conceivably he had gone away, even emigrated. There were some hints that he might have a job abroad, though it was all guesswork. Possibly no more of these killings would take place here or in the county, and there would be no more chances to pick up new leads on him. How long would Barton hang on if things stayed quiet? Could you fit a blue lamp to a Bath chair?

Now and then local papers came up with some fresh speculation about the King Richard murder and even the ones earlier. The nationals had long lost interest, after a period at the end of March when several ran big pieces criticising the police: 'fear stalks the streets unabated', and all that. You couldn't really blame them. Girls from twelve to fourteen were not safe now and it was the job of the police to make them safe.

Lately, Harpur had taken to prowling near girls' schools and youth clubs when they turned the kids out, trying to spot someone hanging about to pick targets. It was hopeless, but nothing else had paid off. Did those sods next door have a real description at last, or maybe something from forensic that could be fed into the computer and bring out one name or two, and not two thousand which was the useless norm here?

When Harpur went back in he saw that Ethan and Lane had moved over to stand near the piano and Iles was talking to their wives and some other women, including Ruth. She looked happy and heart-breakingly out of reach in a flimsy, short flowered dress. It would do him good to be near her for a little while, even in a crowd like this, a bonus on all the other bonuses. He strolled that way. Iles was amusing and charming them with some complicated yarn about the recent troubles of moving his household here. Ruth stood at the edge of the group. For a moment they could talk privately.

'Enjoying yourself?' Harpur asked.

'So, so. You?'

'Now and then. Now.'

'Megan looks very nice.'

'I'll tell her.'

She replied, but Barton had begun to hammer 'The Lambeth Walk', his wife yelling the words. What Ruth said was lost.

'Ah, grand,' Iles cried. 'This will buck us all up.'

Ruth smiled a goodbye and followed the rest over to the piano. Iles did not go. 'Col, I want you to get a good boy, a really good boy, to dig out whatever there is to dig out on Mr Lane.'

'Find what they've got on the Lolita Man, beyond the basics which they're obliged to give us?'

'Well, yes, that. Oh, certainly that. More, though. It's a profile in depth of Lane himself that interests me. I'd like to see his full history. Get somebody just to work through his career, talk to people who knew him when he was a sergeant, that sort of thing. Find some dirt. Christ, Col, do you want him running the shop here?'

'I don't know him, sir.'

'But you know what he is. If they get that kind of foothold – what do you think your future would be like with a Mick at the top? They look after each other and only each other and always each other. In a way, the solidarity is admirable. It's part of their sodding creed, man – their history. I never heard of a Jewish Pope. I'm here for five years, maybe more, as Assistant. I don't want it to be under someone like Lane.'

'I –'

'All right, you'll probably reply that you're in a Force with the Lodge at the top and you're not a Mason. It's a reasonable rejoinder, though you could, of course, soon put that right if you wished. In any case, you've been looked after here, haven't you? You've done all right for your age, surely. Good God, remarkably – chief super at, what, thirty-eight?'

'Thirty-six.'

'Well, there you are.'

'You probably know how that happened, sir. Your predecessor fancied my wife. I'd been thinking of leaving the Force. He wanted me to stay, or her to stay, rather. So he lobbied for me. He had stars in his eyes and I got a crown and star on my shoulder.'

'Yes, well I'd heard about that, of course. I didn't want to intrude on what could be a painful area. Did it amount to much?'

'Who knows? You don't ask a woman that, do you? But I doubt it. Megan doesn't like police, especially brass.'

'So right. She's very perceptive. We're full of arrogance and despair. I mean, look at Cedric Barton, for God's sake. Wonderful backbone and great with a tune, yet a spirit in endless mourning, like a Spanish widow. Those sad, suffering eyes.'

People had begun to dance in lines, arms around each other and kicking their legs out.

'In many ways Lane is a prince,' Iles said, 'bursting with brain and showing some real warmth and what would pass as integrity where he comes from, certainly. His wife's less crude than would appear at first, too. Sure, fat rear, but not to an unacceptable level yet. Give her a month in a health farm and she might come out looking like a sex object and not just an object. What I'd like is for you to assign someone with a known flair for working backwards into the history of a target, able to recognise what can do serious damage. It won't necessarily be corruption or shagging around, but anything that smells a little, even a little, such as far-right politics or a whisper he used to get heavy with prisoners or CND. Anything to affront those lefty fuckers on the Police Authority. We need a good mixture of stuff against him, to alienate enough people. The Authority are all bloody sorts. How else would I have managed to pick up sufficient votes?'

'Jesus, sir, I've got a major brick-wall case on my hands,' Harpur said. 'He's been quiet for a few months, but who knows that's going to last? We've got the Press poised all the time to make a song, and *Newsnight*, *World In Action*, *That's Life* and Rolf Harris. I need all my people, especially my good people.'

'Point taken, Colin. Of course, of course. Would you be offended, though, if I say you think short-term? This is the difference between what one might call board-room level and manager level, even the brightest and most talented manager, such as yourself. Naturally, you are concerned with the immediate menace of the kid killer. It's your responsibility and a grim one. But I have to look ahead and consider the very health and soul of our team in the future. I'm new here, but I like what I see: the enthusiasm, the straightness. Things are done with zest and it is all above board. I feel a duty to guard these qualities. They are what makes us effective, surely, and what might enable us to nail this creature before anyone else, and particularly before the fucking Papes. I say this despite my fears that they are hiding something crucial and are about to make a move. So you see, if we can get some dirt together on Lane and slip it through to the Authority it would be essentially a good and valuable act, a caring act. We'd do the spreading of it to the Authority with subtlety, of course. I can handle it. I've excellent contacts with some of the members.'

Barton had started an encore to his encore. Ruth and Megan were holding each other in one of the dancing groups. Iles watched for a while nodding and beaming with pleasure.

'That's the kind of thing I mean, Col. Your wife and Mrs Avery able to come together like that in unaffected friendship. It's wholesome, no other word will do. Now, who creates the circumstances for this sort of fine *esprit de corps*? Cedric Barton. A big and considerable man is needed to follow such a Chief, Col. After Barton I couldn't work under some bladder like Lane. What would happen to the Force if the two of us were at war?'

Some dancers were tiring. Megan's friend Sybil and her husband, Eric Day, left the floor, pretending to stagger with exhaustion.

'Oh, well done,' Iles declared. 'How are you both? Wonderful food at this do – as always, I'm told. And didn't the Chief mention you had a super-bright daughter? Is it Jennifer? How goes it with her?'

'Fine,' Sybil said.

'Grand,' Iles replied. 'Is she coming into the police, do you think?'

'She'd be handy with the notebook. Always scribbling,' Eric Day said.

'Good for Jennifer,' Iles cried.

'But she's decided not to be Jennifer any longer,' Sybil said. 'Now we have to call her Cheryl-Ann. It's a phase, I suppose.'

'Exactly. I always wanted to be called Beauregard as a kid,' Iles replied. 'Nobody would have it.'

When they were by themselves again, Harpur said: 'Look,

sir, I don't like this – putting a man to burrow into a senior officer's life.'

'I understand your scruples, admire them, believe me. But what I'm suggesting is in the best police traditions, surely. We always bring in an outside officer to investigate a complaint. That's what I'd like to do unofficially here. Think nothing of it, Col. Just get your finger out and organise things, will you?'

'Yes, but –'

'Ah, here's Mrs Avery,' Iles cried, drawing her towards him. 'Well, it's wonderful to see you, Ruth. I'm so pleased you could come and that you look so – so beautiful. Doesn't she, Colin?'

'Certainly.'

'You've made a grand recovery. Colin has been able to give you some aid during these difficult months, I believe.'

She looked startled and glanced at Harpur.

'However busy Col may be on the routines of policing, such as a string of child murders, he can always find an afternoon here or there for those more general, personal responsibilities of a leader. Col is very strong on human relationships, and this is important. We are dealing, after all, with flesh and blood. Col's an exceptionally good flesh man. It should be on his documents.'

The party grew. Barton and his wife joined them, then Megan and Mrs Lane. Barton said: 'I've taken some real refreshment from tonight – from the whole day. We shall all work and serve the better for it. I suppose the public might misunderstand and assume we were neglecting the job. It's not like that. These moments of relaxed friendship count for so very much.'

'Cast thy bread upon the waters,' Mrs Barton stated.

4

25 June

He, wonderful he, is so faithful. Always he is there. Never does he gaze at any other girl. Today, in the tropical heat of the afternoon, he wore a wonderful loose, pleated white shirt, wide open to his neck and chest. His chest is wide and tanned so deeply. I believe he has lately been overseas, perhaps to Peru or Mozambique. Those are lovely names. Although he wears no rings he has a beautiful medallion on a chain around his neck and resting on his wonderfully tanned chest. I believe the medallion has a phoenix bird on it, the bird which is in legend and is magic. It is able to rise from the ashes of a fire and begin life once more. This is a wonderful story, and my life seems to be beginning anew, also. Today, as he was seated at the wheel of the blue Lagonda once again with the registration DE1 the medallion gleamed in the sunlight like true gold on a background of rich velvet.

Nobody would be able to understand what joins wonderful Mr Dark Eyes and me. How could anyone? We are linked in a mysterious fashion. He is more myself than I am. He's always, always in my mind: not as a pleasure, any more than I am always a pleasure to myself, but as my own being.

His hair has been recently modelled, I think. It does not fall forward so far over his forehead as it did before. I believe the new style is extremely attractive, for it seems to mean his wonderful eyes shine out more clearly in his tanned face, which as mentioned previously is unadorned by either beard or moustache. This is one of my few regrets about Mr Dark Eyes.

Soon, I know it, we shall meet and talk and then I shall tell him all my various thoughts, many of them so secret and meant only for him. He, also, will have secret thoughts, and these will be about me, and he will tell them to me. I think he will call me his Cheryl-Ann. This will be the beginning of something new and wonderful and eternal in our lives.

Unfortunately he, wonderful he, smokes cigarettes, I do not know which brand, it may be what is known as low tar, which I hope. Today he smoked while he watched me. Little did Sir Walter Raleigh know of the damage that would be caused when he brought the idea of smoking to our British ancestors in history. In those days it was thought to be a great discovery but later it was found this was not so. When I speak to Mr Dark Eyes I shall ask whether he knows about the bad effects tobacco can have on someone's health, even young, which has been definitely proved. I will ask him if he wants his lungs to become black and thereupon I am sure he will give up smoking cigarettes, which can also stain the teeth and make a person's breath rotten and breath is so important in social gatherings when people are close to each other and being conversational. I shall not refer to the matter of cigarettes immediately but only after we have known each other for a while because it is best to be tactful about this kind of matter. If he has been overseas for some time he may not have heard about the bad effects of tobacco if it was in some remote jungle area or desert, and it will be so helpful for me to inform him and so perhaps save the life of my dearest Mr Dark Eyes.

How I wish he would beckon me to his car. I would go and we could drive to some secret destination, talking together discussing all the matters that those in love guard for each other. Soon I think he will beckon me. He should not fear that I would refuse to go. Perhaps he is a little shy through being abroad, possibly in remote areas of other lands.

5

I am happy again. As I lie here waiting to sleep I can once again rejoice that the search is over. I have found her, a new one. Already I feel content, though I have not even spoken to her yet. I do not think I shall need to take a drink or a pill to sleep tonight.

At first I was not sure she was the right girl. Just by looking from a distance it isn't easy to tell. For many days I've watched her and now I'm suddenly certain, thank God, thank God. I no longer live in that terrible cavern of emptiness and pain. Tonight in my prayers I gave thanks that I have been able to find her among so many. Please God let it be that I do not lose her. Do not send me back to that black pit. Prayer is such a help in my life.

She knows I have watched her, I am sure of this. Now and then she looks at me and our eyes speak, so briefly but enough. I think she is a gentle and kind child. I do hope that this is so. She is not pretty, and this is good. None of them have been pretty. Pretty ones are nice but they know too much. They have been to discos and even to pubs, some of them, despite their age. I don't like that kind. She will be happy that I have noticed her and would like to be close to her. She is a girl who seems often alone and I like that because she will need me.

At present it's enough for me just to look at her and see the signs that she's gentle and kind and wishes to be close to me and help save me from my hell. Does she know that before I found her I lived in such darkness? Yes, yes, she feels that, because she's so sensitive and good, not like all those great gangs of cruel girls who care about nothing but themselves and their clothes and shut themselves away from everyone by wearing earpieces and listening to music. I believe when I ask her to come in the car it will be all right. She will not scream and shout. Their mothers tell them to do that. Most of them have mothers who have forgotten what love is.

Once on the television news a big, hard-looking cop said I must be a very lonely man who needed help. He wanted to tell me that if I got in touch with him down at the bloody Lubianka he would make sure I was given help. Thanks for fuck all. It is not help I need, you big thug, it is love, only love, love from a girl, a girl not too old, a girl really young, a gentle and kind girl from a nice private school with high class navy and red uniform, a girl who has not been playing around with boys, letting them close to her, using foul language. I can't stand that.

What bloody cop is going to understand this? All those sods know about is getting the boot in. Some days I can remember that cop's name, but not now because it's time to sleep. Once

I've seen this thug waiting near the spot where I sometimes station myself to see her. I didn't like that. He looked about a lot but there were many people waiting there and walking by and he did not seem to notice me. How could he notice me? Nobody knows me and I don't get too near the school gates, I know the way she goes home and I can see her there. The cop was talking away into a hidden tape recorder, pretending to be doing nothing. He's as big as a tank but thinks he can stand there and nobody will notice. He was just busy watching all the mothers and fathers, a waste of time. He will never get those big hands on me. I know what I'd do before I let that happen.

It's a long time since the television spoke about me, or the newspapers, not since the King Richard hotel. I don't mind. I don't like the sort of things they say. It might frighten her. But I can see she's not frightened now. Those other days and what the television and newspapers used to say are forgotten. That's much better.

6

This week it was the favourite hotel of both of them on their love circuit but Ruth failed to turn up. Harpur stood in the window and watched the road for her car or lay on the bed in his clothes wondering if what he had long feared was happening now, the fade-out. They were good beds here, king-size doubles which did not squeak or groan or smell of feet. No graffiti or insect blood disfigured the décor. It had always made her feel good to come here: 'Romance, not fornication,' she said once. Only those slimy hints by Iles could have scared her off.

Briefly, in the car-park at the end of the midsummer night's party, Harpur had been able to talk again with her.

'He knows about you and me?' she had whispered. 'You told him?'

'Don't be crazy.'

'Sorry. But some men do.'

'So do some women.'

'Has he had us followed or something? Jesus, Colin, what sort of situation is this?'

'The sod's guessing. Maybe he's seen us talking and put two and two together. Police are good at that. It's to pressure me, love. He wants something dirty done.'

'I'm going to be looking over my shoulder all the time.'

'If we were being tailed I'd know. He'd have to use my own boys, and they'd tell me. It's bluff, Ruth.'

'What sort of dirty job?'

'I'm supposed to collect some smears.'

'You'll do it?' Her voice said she wanted him to, wanted anything that would quieten things down again. It was clear that her worries came not because their affair was known about but because it was known about by Iles. He could understand that.

'You'll do it?' she asked again.

'Probably. Don't let it upset you, Ruth,' he had replied.

'Christ, if it got to Megan – I mean got to Megan through the neat, nasty little mouth of Iles. Can you imagine what it would be like for you, for me, for the kids, yours, mine, your job?'

The intensity surprised him. 'I'm not the first adulterous cop. We usually blame the shift system.'

'I'm a twelve-month widow, Colin. Think about that – widow of a subordinate. Wouldn't we come out of it smelling sweet? I couldn't take that. My kids still think the world of their father. He's a hero to them, and I want that to go on. Please: do it, whatever it is Iles wants. Keep him in check.'

And in a way Brian Avery had been a hero, if trying something bigger than you could handle was heroic. He had done his blundering best to pick up whispers on a planned bank raid, and was killed for it and dumped in the sea. It was the kind of death that needed a bit of a lift.

'I'll do my best,' Harpur had said. And then Megan and Sybil Day and her husband, Eric, had arrived and the conversation with Ruth ended. Perhaps it was not all that had ended.

He left the hotel after an hour and phoned Ruth's house. One of her sons answered and Harpur put the receiver down. The boy might be sick and away from school, so she could not leave him alone. For a moment the thought cheered him. Once before that had happened, without her being able to let him know. His uneasiness did not go away, though. Despite what he had said to Ruth, as he left the hotel and, now, stepping from the telephone booth, he found himself surveying the street with care, looking for someone doing a gumshoe job on him for Iles. There might be people in his department who would take on even that kind of pubic snooping when an ACC wanted it. If you were trained to spy was it such a big step to spy on a mate? There could be lads under him who loathed Harpur. Of course there could be. Christ, who did he think he was, Mr Lovable?

He decided he would take one of his walks, the kind of hopeless patrol he had done so often these last weeks, on the look-out for any random bits of information around a school or youth club that might help with a fraction of a lead to the Lolita Man. The computer did its sophisticated bit, and he would help out with the foot-work. A girls' private school stood not far from where Ruth lived in Canberra Avenue and he half conned himself now that he wanted to look at it. What he really wanted was the possibility of seeing Ruth in the street, or in her window. He passed the end of the avenue on his way to Ash Tree School, but she was not about. Her car stood outside the house.

It was a school he had visited once before and dismissed as a dead loss because more than half the girls were picked up by mummy in a car. A comprehensive like John Locke, where his own daughters went, would offer a far better range. All the same, he hung around the gates as the children came decorously out at the end of another day in their neat red and navy uniforms. Back at the nick a couple of detectives had been ordered to draw up a list of likely future Lolita Man victims. Did they realise that a factor could be the unavailability of either parent to meet the child because both worked? And one-parent kids would be vulnerable for the same reason.

His drill here, or wherever he did his observations, was to look for a car that might seem unconnected to any child and with a man alone inside. Or he scanned the pedestrians for a male face that recurred, yet was not a parent. It couldn't be more sloppy and approximate. To remember a face – just one face on its own – with enough accuracy for identification was a skill as rare as sword-swallowing. Attempting to keep the features of twenty or thirty men in your mind from one week to another was a roaring farce. In any case, the Lolita Man must have had a lot of practice by now at watching his targets and wouldn't get stupidly close. Although there might be something wrong with his mind, he would know the net was out for him.

He could have done with a photographer, but cameras were generally spotted and if that happened these sessions would be useless, even more useless. Note-taking would have been the same. Instead, he used to wire himself up with a tape recorder and spoke the registration numbers into it and descriptions of all the males on show. Afterwards, he would give the numbers to the computer, which always replied with an innocuous tally of kids' parents or people who lived in adjoining houses. As for the descriptions, he wrote them on to cards, his own private little records system, and then tried to match them up.

But what did it mean if some of them did seem to match? Was it relevant to look for a face that kept appearing? Did the Lolita Man watch victims before making his move? One of their cases seemed to say the attacks were spontaneous, the second was inconclusive. At the third, in the King Richard, he would have had time to watch because the girl and her parents had been guests for ten days before she was killed. More details about the two cases in the county would have helped, but that was not on. Ethan and Lane disclosed only the basics, because they could not do less. Were they going to donate extras to a Lodge Force, for Christ's sake?

So, his observations were all sketchy and comically unscientific; but what had science done so far to bring in the poppet hunter and save children's lives?

The girls and the cars dispersed, leaving Harpur alone at the gates, murmuring into his tie-mike the last of disappearing registration numbers. Quite a few very high-priced cars took part in the ferrying, several with personalised plates. Harpur recalled some of these from last time and didn't bother to record them now. As he chattered away there, anyone watching must have wondered whether he was some sort of idiot out on permit, or some sort of raver. Good God, one day a gang of parents might get the wrong idea and he would be lynched. After all, some of these girls were mightily fanciable, even to him with daughters that age, and maybe the interest glinted now and then in his face. The Lolitas could be very winning, very leggy, very ripe. Of course, or there wouldn't be a charming novel about one. And think of that film producer who specialised in little girls: no good trying to explain it away by saying he was foreign. Lust on the march collected all sorts behind its rampant banner, as Iles liked to say.

Yes. He walked towards Ruth's place. Ahead of him a girl of about fourteen from Ash Tree was making her way home alone, clearly in no hurry. At a small crossroads she slowed even more, gazing about as if expecting to see someone special. Whoever it was had said that teenage girls seemed totally unworried about the Lolita Man could have proved their case from this dawdling kid. She turned off towards an estate of big, new houses and Harpur lost sight of her.

From the corner of Ruth's street he saw that her Allegro was still at the kerb. Contrary to everything they had agreed time and again he entered the street now and went its full length, slowing outside her house and gazing in through the windows. He thought he saw someone there but couldn't be sure and certainly couldn't be sure it was Ruth. At the end of the avenue he stopped and turned back. As he passed the house this time he heard her speak to him and saw the front door was half-open.

'I couldn't, Colin. My nerve went.'

He stopped and pretended to tie a shoe lace, the oldest and feeblest trick taught in detective school. 'Are you OK?'

'No, of course I'm not. I've been trying to end it. You shouldn't have come up here.'

She looked and sounded as if she might weep. Harpur said: 'Well, all right, I'll –'

She whispered something, interrupting him, but a car passed in the street, drowning the words.

'What?'

'Oh, please,' she said, and fully opened the door. He realised she must have invited him in. 'For God's sake,' she pleaded.

As soon as she had shut the door behind him her arms were around his neck and her mouth to his. She pulled away and spoke at a rush: 'Colin, it was terrible, knowing you were there alone – and in our best place. Let me pay you something towards the room, such a waste. And it hurt you, too? Still does? For you to come out here – it must really mean a hell of a lot to you, darling.' She was half smiling with pleasure, half crying.

'I rang. Is there a child here?'

'He'd forgotten his trombone. They're at band practice in school.' She kissed him again and shoved both hands inside his jacket. 'What's this?'

He rolled up the recorder wire and mike. In his pocket the handset burbled.

'It's like being propositioned by General Electric,' she said.

'How long before your kids are back?'

'Not long.' She drew him to the stairs.

'We can be quick.'

'I don't like being quick. Who does?'

'Well, quickish.'

There were wedding pictures of her and Avery in the bedroom and a large portrait of him looking resolute when he was a uniformed sergeant. 'These upset you?' she asked, undressing quickly.

'So, so.' The last time he had seen Avery he was lying dead and trussed on the foreshore.

'Sweetheart, I had another life. No use pretending otherwise.'

'I know.'

In a while, though, she said: 'They really have done you damage, haven't they?'

'Something has.'

'Did I ever know such a sensitive pig?' She left the bed and put the pictures face down. Then, after a time, she said: 'Darling, darling, what a bonny recovery. I'll remember next time.'

'Next time?'

'You've been to the house now. You came searching for me. I like that. The step's been taken and let Iles go fuck himself.'

'This is better.'

'As good as anything I've ever had.'

'Only as good?'

'We can work on it. Could you come in through the garden in future? There are a couple of old biddies who spend their time watching the street from their windows.'

Before leaving he stood the photographs up again.

At the nick there was a message for him to see Barton immediately and when Harpur arrived at the Chief's room he found Iles there, too. Both looked sick, especially Iles. Barton sat at his desk while Iles paced about, snarling.

'Colin, we have some grand news,' Barton said. 'It's possible our kiddies may be safe again. The word is that Ethan and Lane have somebody inside for the girl jobs.' His voice trembled slightly like a child reporting a bad exam result to his parents.

'They've had him in for hours,' Iles added. 'It looks bad.'

He must mean they might have the right man. 'How much of this is official?' Harpur asked.

'Oh, absolutely bugger all,' Iles replied. 'They're not going to tell us anything, at this stage, are they?'

'So how do we know they haven't made a mistake?' Harpur asked.

'We don't – not a hundred per cent,' Iles said. 'But it sounds pretty good. They've been building up to it. This is not a rush job.'

'Description? Name?'

'Come on, Col. Are we likely to be told that until they've got it all parcelled up?'

'I don't understand how we know about it then.'

'It comes from a BBC man,' Iles explained. 'I was at a road safety affair. Their reporter had a phone call and came back and asked me what I knew about the guy they'd picked up next door. He said they were busy seeing he squared with their dates and so on, and doing damn well. I'd been expecting something, as you know, but it hit the wind out of me. Naturally, I made out I'd had a whisper. What sort of twats do we look otherwise, Col – like those bloody Nips in the jungle still fighting the war in 1960? I take it you haven't heard anything?'

'I've been casing a school.'

Iles nodded: 'Dinky tits on some of those fourth formers.'

Barton muttered, 'Well, all that could be superfluous in the circumstances. It does look very watertight. Thank God it may all be over.' He sounded stricken and miserable.

'They'll have to inform us,' Harpur said. 'We've got to question him on our three. It won't do just being able to line him up with their cases.'

'When they feel like it they'll inform us,' Iles replied. 'And that will be after charges, I'd bet. That pair of operators, Ethan and Lane, will probably have their pictures in the paper shaking hands with each other. Remember that Yorkshire Ripper press conference? *Gloire, gloire, gloire.* Pray see how smart we are. Are they going to let us in on that? Are they fuck. There's a gong in this for Ethan – gallant and timely slayer of the buggering dragon. Plus a scroll from the Vatican. Illuminated. We're going to be a small-type footnote to this case, let in when the whole thing's played out and shattered, like number twenty-five in a gang bang.'

Barton coughed a bit. 'Myself, I don't feel we should blame ourselves unduly. They appear to have had exceptional luck, something that either comes or doesn't. Throughout my career I've noticed the importance of the rub of the green.'

Iles rolled his eyes.

'I'm inclined to be a little more relaxed about this than Desmond.' The Chief smoothed his long face reflectively with two fingers of his left hand. A thick gold wedding band sparkled like a hypnotist's prop. 'I'm intent on looking on the bright side,' he stated, 'concerned above all with the wonderful possibility that no more children will be murdered.'

'Granted, sir,' Iles said, softening his voice at once. He walked behind the Chief's chair and staring at Barton's back crossed himself ferociously, a gesture Harpur had seen him use before, and one that Iles would regard as the most abusive in his locker. 'I'd be the last to argue that they've pulled this off by skill. The resemblances with the Ripper case are pressing: total fluke plus a decent slice of initiative by low-rank officers.'

'What happened?' Harpur asked.

'Botched attempt on a girl yesterday evening,' Iles replied. 'Apparently they've had a couple of incidents like it lately –

failed assaults, as if the Lolita Man were getting careless. Not enough injury to compel them to report it. They were just waiting for it to happen again on their patch. That's why they were bloody smug at the cricket do. They had everything keyed up, ready for the next move.'

'There was a hue and cry after yesterday's incident,' Barton said. 'Then he disappeared.'

'They got him in Cawston Woods this morning,' Iles continued. 'Dogs, a battalion of men, the lot. Mobile fucking canteen, hot soup for the lads. Like the Second Front. It's going to be all over the telly. Did Ethan sell tickets?'

'This is press information again, Col. We must be fair. Things may not have been quite like that.'

'Oh, of course, sir,' Iles said. 'Forgive my little jet of venom. One shows anger only as the flint bears fire – a hasty spark and straight is cold again. In their way they are a very capable team, Ethan and Lane, and not uncharming with it. Lane a fine tenor, I believe, and notable in light opera. As you say, sir, let us not begrudge them their success. The Micks' turn today, perhaps ours on something else before long. That, after all, is policing.'

Barton, looking confused by Iles's change of tone, raised his old head like a worn-out pointer and sniffed for piss-taking. It cost him a lot of effort to keep up with the ACC and there were times lately when he did not bother to try. He shrugged now.

'Why should the Lolita Man suddenly start making errors?' Harpur asked. 'He's always been a perfectionist. The man they've got could be just some small-time, routine gym-slip groper.'

'Good boy, Col. I admire optimism,' Iles said.

'Have we contacted them?' Harpur asked.

'We consider that move must come from Vincent Ethan,' Barton replied gravely. 'Desmond and I are in total accord on this.'

'Technically, we still know nothing of what has occurred, Col. You see our difficulty, I'm sure.'

'A protocol matter, and more than a protocol matter,' Barton said.

'Exactly, sir,' Iles remarked.

'How more than protocol, sir?'

'All kinds of implications, Colin,' Barton replied.

'All kinds,' Iles said.

'I won't bore you with that now,' Barton added.

Iles in shirt-sleeves sat on the corner of the Chief's big desk, as if the two were budding tycoons posing for a picture in *Business News*. 'Put it like this, Col. Can you see me or the Chief crawling like a couple of scroungers to ask Ethan and Lane if they would be gracious enough to give us a sniff of their sodding loaves and fishes? What would be our actual words? "I understand – Vincent, Mark – though I am by no means sure of my facts – that you may have brilliantly nicked someone for the girl killings. We would be perpetually grateful for any information, and so pleased if eventually – in your own good time, naturally – you allow us brief access to this gifted violater."'

'Ethan always wanted to go to the Inspectorate of Constabulary,' Barton said with a harsh sigh, like someone left yards behind in the race, yet still flogging himself.

'So, if Ethan makes it to the Inspectorate we could have him poking around here soon, telling us how to run the shop,' Iles said. 'Jesus. And by that time, Lane could be in your post as Chief, sir. Do we just roll over and let them gut us?'

Barton shrugged again. 'I'm happy to say we have nothing to hide here, Desmond.'

'Of course, not, sir,' Iles replied. 'But I can't bear to think of Lane in your mahogany-panelled personal toilet. It's a matter of scale. We're used to a big man leading us.'

When Harpur and Iles left the Chief they went to the ACC's room. 'I've been doing some telephoning around myself on that little commission I gave you, Colin.'

'Lane's form?'

Iles removed a book lying open in an easy chair, so Harpur could sit down. '*Vanity Fair*,' Iles snorted. 'God, what those old scribblers could get away with. Lane – yes. He was an undergraduate at Warwick, but I don't necessarily hold that against him; I knew quite a decent chap who was at Hull. Lane won office in the union and in the Conservative Students' Association there. He was quite a star. This would be around 1960. There's a story about vote rigging for one of these posts. Your man could find out very easily what went on – there'd be minutes and so on. The poll in question was a straight fight between him and a black and Lane came out best. Of course. We might be able to make something of this, Col. Two strands: the chicanery and the colour, but especially the colour. Apparently our friend was altogether a bit suspect on race matters in those days, not National Front or anything indiscreet, but pro immigration controls, that sort of thing.

'You see, Colin, this whole situation has become more urgent if they really have got the Lolita Man. Lane's going to be up there on a pedestal with Ethan, isn't he? But if we can spread it that he's not one hundred per cent for the sooties we'll soon shake the image. There are people on our Authority who wouldn't give a shit if we never caught a crook as long as we were nice to Rastas. You know how multi-racialist we are here. Do we want a white-supremacy careerist jackbooting about among our admirable Afro-Carib brethren down Dolphin Road and so on? You've got some first-class black contacts, haven't you, Col? That Rev. with the Balliol accent and the suits. Anstruther? Witch doctor at the Church of the Free Gospel, or whatever. Put a word in his sensitive ear. It will reach his congregation and we'll be on our way. Let the seed fall on good ground and it will multiply, yea, an hundred fold. Tell the Rev. you're worried about the chance of all the carefully constructed race relations apparatus here being fatally kicked in the goolies by Heinrich Lane, if he gets the job. You see the picture?'

'Is it –?'

'Is it right to be messing about on career objectives when we have a major case involving the death of kids? You always put your finger on things unerringly, Col, unerringly. My reply would be that the case could now be closed. And, second, you'll find in all jobs that it is people's careers which take precedence over everything else, even if they are handling world shattering events. Look at Churchill. All right, the Second World War rates as big stuff, but don't tell me it was as big to him as getting back into Number 10. People's work and status is their core, Col. I'm sure you know it.'

'It seems so –'

'Malevolent? I don't want you to think I'm gunning for Lane out of spite. Nor that this is just a crude Lodge against Papal

State matter. If there's one thing I despise it's bigotry. But I think you know that. What I fear is that we could have a re-run of the inner-city riots here, should someone crude like Lane take over. I see an admirably harmonious relationship between the races in our area – no credit to me, I've been here less than two years. How sad though if it were all jeopardised.'

'I –'

'Put someone young and subtle on it, would you, Col, someone who wants to go places fast. If it embarrasses you, he can report to me. I don't mind being seen to care for this Force.'

'I'd prefer it like that.'

'No problem.' He opened *Vanity Fair*. 'You won't ever speak about this, will you?'

'Lane?'

'No, no. I've just said I've no objection to that being known. But don't put it around that I read this kind of old garbage.' His intercom buzzed and the Chief spoke from the machine. Iles did an elaborate bow to the voice and turned up the volume for Harpur to hear.

'Desmond, Vince Ethan has just been on. I'm invited over for informal talks with him this evening about their arrest and how we play things jointly from now on. This is to do with interrogations and such like over the next few days. Strictly *à deux* for the moment. I see it as an unexpectedly decent gesture on his part, and I've accepted, of course.'

Iles mimicked a grateful curtsey.

'Vince says we won't be able to interview the prisoner until tomorrow evening at the earliest. They're still hard at it with him themselves. He's denying everything.'

'They'll need twenty-four hours to put his nose and kidneys back in the right places before anyone from outside sees him,' Iles said.

'Vincent sounds full of confidence.'

'Sir, what he's full of is shit.'

'Can you get in touch with Harpur and tell him to hold himself in readiness for an interrogation session over there late tomorrow? I don't want him disappearing on one of his cock jousts.'

Iles glanced apologetically towards Harpur. 'I'll make sure

he's warned. In any case, for liaisons he's one of the afternoon men, a giddy-head.'

'How's that?'

'A quote from *The Anatomy of Melancholy*, sir.'

'That a book? Make a hell of a good title for my memoirs. Pity it's been used.' The Chief signed off.

'Notice Ethan's become Vince all at once, Col? Buddies. Nobody's a better loser than the Chief.'

In his own room Harpur worked for a while on possible sighting reports of the Lolita Man going back to the first incident. They were a mess, a jumble. The ages ranged from eighteen to forty-five, the hair colour spectrum from bleached to jet, though with the balance just in favour of dark. A few said he had exceptionally luminous, dark eyes, probably a wow with schoolgirls, if this really was the Lolita Man. As to physique he might be five foot eight or six foot two and his weight was somewhere between eleven and fourteen stone. At least they all said he was Caucasian and nobody had seen a beard, though some reported a moustache. If Ethan and Lane really had a likely candidate, but one who wouldn't cough, some of these descriptions could turn out important very soon in the attempts to nail him.

He would have liked to see all reports of supposed sightings in the county, too. Some constants might then have emerged. As it was, next door supplied only enough material to increase the stack of contradictions and dead-ends already available. The poor bugger running the regional crime squad operation would be right for certification after dealing with the two Forces on this one.

Harpur shuffled the cards around on his table. For himself, he was coming to prefer the basic shoe-leather sort of detection to all these nicely typed, clashing bits of documentation. The long gaps between some attacks might suggest the Lolita Man left the area for set spells, and this had led to theories that he worked elsewhere, maybe abroad. There had been half-hearted checks on men with jobs on oil rigs or deep-sea vessels, but the information was sketchy and not collated anywhere.

The tendency had been to assume he was single and working-class. Why, though? A lot of rapists seemed happily married, with plenty of normal sex on offer. They liked the struggle. This boy liked the struggle to the point of slaughter, which made him very special: as Iles said, he would get into the textbooks. He could be special in other ways, too. There had to be a chance he was well-off, perhaps leisured, or with businesses abroad that required his presence every so often for a long while. Why assume knocking off young girls was confined to Labour voters? What was that other Iles *mot*, about the mixture who marched behind the rampant banner of lust?

He gathered up the cards and put them away, defeated. On the whole he agreed with the sentiments Barton had forced himself to speak, against all his instincts and prejudices, and in the face of Iles's contempt. Harpur, too, would be glad if the county really had cracked this one. He had meant it when he told the two of them that he could not face looking at any more murdered children.

He feared he might have to, though. It sounded to him as if Ethan and Lane had the wrong boy. The Lolita Man wasn't somebody who suddenly grew daft and careless and found himself on the wrong end of a hue and cry. Harpur's dread remained that the timetable said another attack must be about due, an attack by the authentic Lolita Man, not some apprentice.

7

27 June

He, wonderful he, was there again today and our eyes met once more in silent contact. Did he look anxious about some matter I know not of? Were his lovely dark eyes even darker through worry and strain? What can be troubling him? Would I could go to him and ask! Perhaps soon. It makes me very sad to see him upset and to have no means to comfort him. It is possible that his business interests abroad in such places as Mozambique and

Peru are causing him large problems owing to various international factors, this is often the case with business.

Today, he wore a black and red rose-printed shirt. I feel sure it is by Monix and is something like the one I have seen Reg Prescott, the pianist in Harvey and the Wallbangers, wear. This was extremely nice and went so well with his great tan and with the gold phoenix medallion. It is obvious he has been abroad recently, it could be to St Trope, as it is known, or Malaga, the rich playboys' special place, there is no Butlins there. Again he was in the beautiful Lagonda, a car which suits his strong features so wonderfully.

It was on television tonight that this morning the police caught a man who attacked a girl. This is good news. People have worried a great deal about this man, if it is the man who has attacked other girls and even killed them. I worried a little but I didn't ever let it show. If I had told mummy about he wonderful he watching me I know she would have thought he could be the man the police have been searching for. I think her favourite word is 'dangerous'. It is because she knows so many police in her work, I expect.

But now all is all right because the real man has been caught and will not be able to do any more attacks and killings. It shows how silly it would have been to think Mr Dark Eyes was such a person.

Oh, would he did not smoke. Again he was smoking today as he sat at the wheel of his Lagonda. I shall tell him this will stain his beautiful hands. Possibly he has not thought of this and the well-known fact that it will make him cough, especially as he grows older. The years ahead are quite important. Perhaps he is smoking more now because he is worried about something, such as his various business interests in other lands. Many smoke owing to worry. It is a kind of drug. But what is he worried about? It cannot be worry about my loyalty to him for always when our eyes meet in silent contact I am able to say with my eyes that he's always, always in my mind: not as a pleasure, any more than I am always a pleasure to myself, but as my own being.

8

Something bad happened today and now when I try to go to sleep I can't because this bad fact is in my head and gives me big aggro.

That big, hard cop was there again today, the big dumbo who was on the television news once asking me to go to him for help, like hell I will. I've remembered his name from the television now. It is Detective Chief Superintendent Colin Harpur, one of the bosses, but just a wooden-top like all the rest. They think they know everything but all they think is dirt, not love and sweetness ever.

Today he was at the school. This is the second time. Why did he come back there? And when she came out from the school the ape walked behind her on her way home. He walked behind her, only her, nobody else, like he was guarding her. Is he a guard? What I don't understand is how he could know which girl I've been looking at. Maybe this sod is not so dim as he looks. This is why I'm awake, I suppose. I will need something to calm me down and make me sleep tonight. There are two big questions. Why did this lump come back to Ash Tree School and why did he follow only her?

Of course, I do not go too near the school gates, that would be so stupid. He is standing there staring about and talking into his bloody pocket recorder all the time, car numbers, I bet, and men's faces. That's how the bastards work. Then they go through it all bit by bit and try to fit things together. They've got a computer to help them, but a computer is not magic. I keep out of his sight. He hasn't got me on his records.

She didn't talk to him. She didn't seem to know he was there, and when she looked at me it was the same as before, that nice way our eyes meet and our eyes seem to speak to each other, full of love. If she had told this big thicko or his people about me I think she would have seemed different from before. She didn't seem ashamed or sly. I'd be very angry and disappointed if she informed the police about us. I don't believe she'd betray things like that. She's only a young girl, not some grown-up woman or wife who is used to double-crossing all the time and used to pretending everything is nice and all right. This is why I like her, because she's young and nice, not a deceitful cow. That's why I liked the others as well, and in the end I had to make sure they didn't grow up and become two-timers like all the others. I had to make sure of that, it's obvious.

But if she hasn't told the police she has noticed me how could they know about her and the school? The thing about police is they might not be stupid all the time, only most of the time. The TV news said those other police have caught someone who did something to a young girl. It didn't say what. He must be stupid and obvious or they would not have caught him. They said police were asking him questions about other incidents so I suppose they think he is me. I don't like that, because he must be dim.

I won't go back to the same place to watch her in case Harpur starts looking there. What I will do is watch her secretly for a while, but I must see her. When I saw that big thug Harpur with her today I didn't like it. He was getting very close, until she went towards her house. Maybe he was thinking of getting his big thick hands on her young body. A lot of these cops are like that, full of dirty sex. They haven't got enough to do. They're supposed to be watching someone, but they turn it into dirty sex instead. He might take her away from me. Oh, God, I'd be back in that deep tomb alone. I feared so much that he'd go close to her that I followed him in the car, but he went up Canberra Avenue and then came back. I don't know where he went then. I had to keep driving. When I passed him he was stopped outside a house pretending to tie his shoe. I didn't understand that. When I looked at his face earlier there was sex in it, like someone thinking about sex, I could see that. It was bloody disgusting. Sometimes I think I've waited too long with this girl, just watching, staying far back, only eyes meeting.

Now, she needs me to look after her properly, she's so gentle and nice. Now this big pig thinks he's going to get on top of her sweet little body. That's all they think about when they're not twisting people's arms and lying about them to the court, it's well known. They think they can have anyone they want. How can I sleep if I think of that gentle, kind child looking into that big face full of dirty sex? I am the only one who can save her. I haven't done enough for her, only watching. It is time.

9

Barton called another little meeting next morning to report on his talks with Ethan. 'Yes, they're sure,' he said. 'An atmosphere of considerable optimism obtains over there, though they are being decently restrained and responsible. No forensic or prints, but apparently they have descriptions from their two incidents and some of them fit this lad.'

'Not descriptions they've let us hear about,' Iles grunted.

'Vincent explained that they were very vague, and in some cases conflicting. Like our own, for God's sake.'

'Yet theirs are OK now to nail the suspect,' Iles said. 'Christ, was dear Vincent taught by Jesuits?'

'You're hard on them, Desmond. In my view they're playing it straight. Pretty straight, anyway.'

'Well, if you say so, sir, of course. I accept your judgement. You must be right. It would be intolerable, after all, to imagine that senior men sat on information which might have saved children's lives.'

Barton allowed himself a moment to analyse the tone of this. Then he said: 'It's not the dark, almost swarthy, man we've been looking for. We could have been very seriously adrift on that, Colin. Not a sliver of blame on you – you have to accept what witnesses give you. But that's how it is.' He read from a typed sheet: 'This guy is five foot eight, slight, with thick, mousy hair, sort of semi-punk, no scars, features small and rounded. Vincent wouldn't provide a picture in case we flashed it around and prejudiced identification parades.'

'Mr Bloody-Whiter-than-White,' Iles stated.

'It's not an unreasonable point,' the Chief said, 'though I took it slightly amiss that he thought we might be so foolish.' He sighed. 'There's been a change of timetabling, Colin. They're not ready for you to see him as soon as they had thought. You won't be needed for an interrogation session tonight after all. You can go home and play Halma with Megan. They'll charge him today with this latest incident, the failed attack, on which they've got him cold, apparently. He'll come up in court tomorrow and they'll ask for a remand in police custody. Then they – and we – can work on tying him to the five killings. So it could be tomorrow evening or the weekend before we get a chance. It's a good dodge – gives everyone more time.'

'Did Ethan let you see him, sir?' Iles asked.

'No, he was undergoing interrogation while I was there. But I'm assured he is in no way damaged, except for a little bruising that resulted from –'

'Resisting arrest,' Iles offered.

'Resisting arrest,' the Chief said. 'Ethan explained the size of the chase: they were afraid he might get caught by members of the public and injured or worse. You know how self-righteous and frothy people become over sex crimes on kids.'

'Really it was a mission of mercy then, sir – the dogs and so on,' Iles remarked.

'Look, Desmond, they've got to bring him into court tomorrow. They wouldn't risk that, would they, if he looked like the raid on Dresden?'

'I suppose they could say he inadvertently stumbled on the way to the cells,' Iles replied. 'There's a lot of inadvertent stumbling these days.'

'I've got his name and address here,' Barton said. 'No previous. He's twenty-three – exactly right for your standard rapist, I think. Medical history of violence as a kid. Married, so sex available, but he must like the resistance and screams. Some people do get very bored with what's on a plate at home, wouldn't you say?'

He looked at Harpur, who did not reply.

'He's textbook stuff,' Barton continued, 'Boston Strangler again, except he picks kids.'

'Yes, all very tidy,' Iles said.

'The description fits one of ours, doesn't it, Colin?'

'Yes. There's a mousy-haired youth on the cards. That was at the King Richard.'

'So, worth some renewed digging there now,' Barton said.

'Possibly. This could focus things. We might be able to stir some recollections,' Harpur replied. 'My own feeling is still that the dark man with the eyes is –'

'Frankly, I'm glad for Vince,' the Chief remarked, 'and that the well-being of the populace at large has been advanced and perhaps secured.'

In the corridor, Iles said: '"Well-being of the populace at large." Has he been listening to Kinnock or is he doing sociology with the Open University on the quiet?'

With Francis Garland Harpur drove out to the King Richard in the afternoon. It was a place he had come to loathe because the memory of the child's torn corpse in the plush room would not leave him. Somehow it had been worse than seeing those earlier two raped young bodies in the open, part-shrouded by bushes and tall weeds, even though those two had cruel rope marks on their wrists and legs. Harpur had found it frightening at the King Richard that the Lolita Man would have the nerve to go inside, saunter past people on his way in and out, and hang about before, doing his spotting.

And then there had been the need for a place like the motel to keep going, to pretend nothing had happened. The King Richard had to protect its image as a sedate and select watering hole. He understood that. A couple of days after the girl died, that room would be let again, perhaps to someone else with a teenage daughter. Even on the day of the murder things had gone on at the hotel pretty much as usual, and the foyer had been bristling with good luggage, golf bags and loud, cheerful voices when the on-call undertaker arrived. It was stupid to feel upset about that, but Harpur had been angry, and resentment with the King Richard lingered. Today, it would be all high spirits and luncheon baskets there again.

The unmarked Ital looked exceptionally crowded. Garland drove with Harpur alongside and, on the back seat, jammed close together and impassive, like shackled prisoners, sat four tailor's dummies. Their wigs ranged from blonde to deepest black.

'I hate the way the one with the moustache hogs the conversation,' Garland said.

When they stopped at lights, Harpur was aware of other motorists staring in, bemused by the sight of these motionless passengers. They were an Iles idea, something that had once worked for him, or half worked, when he was running CID in the North-West. The dummies had been made to look like the four most recurrent descriptions of the Lolita Man: features, clothes, build, colouring, hair. Iles ordered that each of them should be put in turn near the site of an attack, to stir local memories. He had wanted the media to do pictures, but the dummies had arrived only this morning and Press and television were uninterested now in four clashing alternatives when next door had a man about to be charged.

Iles had watched Harpur and Garland load the car with the four replicas, and Harpur noticed, as he had noticed before today, that Iles showed a special coldness towards Garland. It was a mystery. Garland could be pushy and impatient but he rated as one of the brightest, hardest-working people around. Perhaps Iles considered him a bit too bright. Garland might be more grist to his paranoia.

At the King Richard Garland asked: 'Start with the mousy-haired punk?'

'I suppose so.'

'Don't believe in it?'

'Do you?'

'So who have they got in the county?'

'An imitator, maybe – someone excited by the accounts of the attacks and wanting a slice.'

They set up the dummy near a side door where they believed the Lolita Man had entered and left. He wore jeans and a suede jacket, and they arranged him facing the door, as if about to sneak in. Its lifelessness seemed to make the figure even more sinister, perversion sculpted for keeps into nicely clothed fibreglass.

The boiler man and a woman cleaner who had seen the unaccounted-for punk on the day of the attack and given

46

the descriptions said the model was a great likeness, but in the wrong place. They had seen the man near bungalows in the grounds, on the other side of the hotel and far away from the girl's room. Few other recollections flowed from the rest of the staff. So, this untraced man had certainly been about on the day, but there was no way yet of linking him with the killings. He could have been anything: sneak-thief, someone's secret lover or just one of the several untraced guests.

Harpur stuck at it, all the same. He and Garland took an elderly chambermaid back to the linen room on the second floor where she had been working on the day in March and they gazed down from a window on to the dummy. She shook her head. 'I seen nobody like that,' she said. 'I would remember him. We don't get many like that.' Bored with the whole thing she was about to turn away but glanced towards the car-park and then looked more intently.

'What is it, Gwen?' Garland asked.

'In the car,' she replied, shading her eyes.

'Which?'

She pointed towards the Ital.

'Yes?' Garland said.

'The man in the back.'

The darkest-haired dummy was seated in profile against the rear window of the car on this side.

She squinted behind her brown horn-rims. 'I often seen a man like that, black hair down across his forehead.'

'When was this?'

'A while ago.'

'Before the killing?'

'Yes, I think so.'

'Just before?' Harpur asked.

'It could be.'

'How often did you see him?' Garland said.

'A good few days. He seemed to be hanging about.'

'From this window?'

'Yes, I'm in here a lot.'

'What was he doing?'

'Not doing nothing. Just staring.'

'Up this way?'

'Yes, this way. I used to be scared he saw me watching him.'

'Why scared, Gwen?' Harpur asked.

'Oh, I don't know. He didn't seem the right sort.'

'For what?'

'Fishy.'

'Could he have been watching the window where the girl stayed?' Garland said.

'Well, yes, he could.'

'And he looked just like that man out there?' Harpur asked, 'no moustache or glasses or beard?'

'No, like that.'

'And he was in a car?' Garland said.

'Always.'

'In the back?'

'No, no, of course not. In the driving seat. There wasn't nobody with him.'

'What make of car?' Harpur asked.

'I don't know nothing about cars, sir. Not like that one he's in now. Bigger. Is he to do with it, then? Why's he out there now? Why don't you go and get him, not just stand talking here?'

'What colour, Gwen?' Garland said.

'How do you mean?'

'The car.'

'It's so long ago. Blue? Yes, might be blue.'

Harpur was turning up the original description of the dark-haired man. 'He wasn't reported from here at all. This came from the first death, the thirteen-year-old – Sharon, at Spring Lane. Seen by three witnesses. A couple of them mentioned the eyes: exceptionally deep and intense.'

'It's too far,' Gwen said.

Harpur brought a chair for her. She was tall and burly, in a white coat too tight for her, and had begun to sweat under the strain of so many questions.

'You didn't mention this man when we asked in March about any odd people, Gwen,' Garland said.

'Well, I thought it was in the hotel you meant, didn't I? The girl was killed in the main hotel building. The car-park – well, always all sorts out there. I can't take account of that, can I?

Have I done something wrong? I'd be sorry if I done something wrong. I don't want no bother with police.'

'No, of course not,' Harpur told her gently. 'Now, this is way back in March, but can you remember what he was wearing?'

She passed a hand over her face and looked beaten by this problem. Gwen would be about the Chief's age and the resemblance did not stop there. She stood up and looked towards the Ital again. 'It could be like he's got on now.'

'Grey leather jacket,' Harpur read from the description notes, 'open shirt, no certainty as to colour, possibly jeans, possibly brown sandals, possibly a medallion, possibly gold, with a bird motif.'

'I don't know about all that. Sandals? I couldn't see, nor no medallion.'

'He was always in the car when you saw him, Gwen?' Harpur asked.

'That's why I didn't take no account of it.'

'Yes, of course.'

'And what about age?'

'Oh, young.'

Harpur waited. For her young could be anything up to forty-five.

'Not thirty. Twenty-eight?'

'We have around twenty-six,' Garland said.

'It's a distance from here. Might be twenty-six. Is he to do with it, then?' she asked again. 'And I was looking at him like that? And now here again?'

'Would you say he was built like the man out there now?' Harpur said.

She had remained at the window. 'Not fat. Yes, like him. Not fat, not skinny. Quite strong. Well, he broke the little thing's neck, didn't he?'

'We don't know that, Gwen,' Harpur replied. 'We don't know for sure whether there's any connection. Some people say it was a man who looked quite different from this – like the punk model we showed you. So don't think about what happened in the room to the girl, just tell us what you recall. You'd say he was powerfully built, would you?'

49

She nodded. 'Pretty good. He looked like he kept in training, if you know what I mean.'

'Yes. And did you tell anyone about him at the time – last March?' Garland asked.

'Well, I wouldn't, would I? He didn't seem of no importance.'

'Day after day in the car-park?'

'We gets all sorts. It's a motel, isn't it – bungalows, chalets, as well as the main part. People all over. I'm not a cop, you know.'

'Did anyone else see him?' Garland said. 'Talk about him?'

'Not to me.'

Harpur helped her up. 'I'm going to get my colleague here to bring you some pictures of cars. You might be able to say if any of them look like the one he was in. Or he could take you to a multi-storey.'

'Big is all I know.'

'Yes, we'll get pictures of big cars,' Harpur said.

'And probably blue,' Garland added.

'Always the same car?' Harpur asked.

She paused. 'It's so long. I think so, but a car's a car to me, that's the trouble.'

'And have you ever seen it or seen him since the death of the girl?' Harpur said.

'I don't think so. Only today.' She sensed this was important, and that a firm answer would be better. 'No.' She stared out at the Ital again and seemed to realise suddenly it was another dummy, perhaps because of the stillness, perhaps because Harpur and Garland did not go after him. 'Oh, I see.'

'We'd really like to know if he ever came back,' Garland prodded.

'No, definite.'

'Fine,' Harpur said. 'You've been great.' He and Garland brought the dark-haired figure, slickly dressed in its bomber jacket and jeans, and placed it near what had been the girl's room. All the staff were summoned and looked at it there, but nobody responded. They had already been asked and asked again about an intruder looking like this.

'So what did Gwen see?' Garland asked Harpur.

'She saw somebody, all right, and time after time. But did he ever come in? A dark private eye doing some divorce snooping?'

The manager began to grow uneasy at having obvious heavies like Harpur and Garland, plus a couple of window display zombies, crowding his guests. The King Richard was still trying to pretend that what had happened hadn't happened, and this session of macabre theatre hardly helped. Early in the evening Harpur gave up and they drove back with their four rigid passengers.

'Ethan and Co. could have it right or could be making one hell of a balls,' Harpur said.

'Iles will like the uncertainty.'

'Not a bad scheme of his, the dummies. He's no fool.'

'I don't think I've ever heard him called that, sir. Other things, never a fool.'

'He seems to dislike you. Ever do anything with his wife?'

'She was a bit lost when they first arrived. And he's rather anti-sex.'

He might have something there. 'What bothers me is that the Lolita Man could be cooking something right now, while everyone thinks it's over. He's quite a schemer. He'll see the chance. If our dark-locked friend in the big blue car is really the one we should be looking for, where do we expect him next? Christ, I wish we'd got further with our list of likely targets. About the only constants are the age group and the fact that none of these kids is pretty or doing much with boys. He must like them shy, in need of attention. How do we cover all the kids like that, for God's sake?'

'It would be a giggle if the next one was in the county, while they're still holding that lad.' Garland must have sensed at once that the phrasing angered Harpur. 'Not a giggle, sir. I didn't mean that. This is the death of a child. A terrible irony, is what I wanted to say.'

'Iles will be holding early morning prayer meetings to demand it should happen, if you'd like to attend.'

On the last Thursday of every month Megan ran a discussion group at the house, mostly for neighbours and people she met through the John Locke parent-teacher association, but also anyone else she could interest. There was a session under way in their front room when Harpur arrived home that evening, and a couple of cars in the road which he did not recognise. Sometimes he went in, to show willing, and he listened at the door tonight for several minutes, wondering whether he would join them. A woman speaker seemed to be giving a paper on the significance of sexual impotence in literature. 'How is it, you may ask, that in two books published at virtually the same time, *Lady Chatterley* and Hemingway's *The Sun Also Rises*, loss of full manhood can be treated in one case as a damning blight and in the other as a factor in the hero's greatness?'

He decided against and took a can of Coke and the evening paper into the garden. His two daughters and a girl he did not know, but seemed vaguely to recognise, were sunbathing on the grass in bikinis, and he sat near them in a deckchair.

'Look out, it's the Old Bill,' Jill said.

'This is Jennifer, only you've got to call her Cheryl-Ann,' Hazel told him.

'Ah, yes, I know her mum,' Harpur replied.

'Well, her mum's in with the eggheads,' Hazel said. 'Our mum press-ganged her, poor thing.'

'What do you think of Cheryl-Ann as a name, dad?'

'Nice. Musical.'

'We like it, too,' Jill said.

'Jennifer's a bit Radio 4, isn't it?' Hazel suggested.

'We're invited back to Cheryl-Ann's one day. They've got a pool. We can snorkel.'

'Great,' he said.

Cheryl-Ann was lying on her back, one arm shielding her face from the sun. She seemed embarrassed by the conversation and had turned her head away from Harpur, so that the neck angle looked awkward. For a moment he found himself glimpsing again that child on the bed in the King Richard. Cheryl-Ann was the same build, a little gangly, starting to develop, with very white skin and fragile-looking knees, like a foal's. Jesus, if he was looking for a kid to protect, this could be one.

'Daddy, you shouldn't stare,' Hazel told him.

No, he shouldn't. 'I thought I recognised the bikini, that's all.'

'I lent her one.'

'Ah.' It bothered him in a strange, foolish way: for this child to wear his daughter's clothes seemed to make the two girls interchangeable, and for no reason at all he had been thinking of Cheryl-Ann as a victim.

'Mummy's pleased with the turn-out tonight,' Jill remarked.

'The Madam Harpur soirée,' Hazel said.

Megan's parents had run the same sort of sessions in Highgate and the habit came naturally to her. Harpur liked the idea, and learned something whenever he looked in. It was probably through the discussion group that Dobson, Iles's predecessor, had struck up whatever it was he had struck up with Megan. Had it died when he left? Since then she had taken to occasional day-long shopping excursions to London. Previously, shopping had always bored her insensible.

'D'you know, dad, that at Cheryl-Ann's school the teachers wear gown things like in *Goodbye, Mr Chips* and the headmistress goes shooting pheasants and similar?' Jill said.

'Your head told me he was thinking of learning how to shoot, for self-defence,' Harpur replied. 'Which school are you at, Cheryl-Ann?'

She spoke from under her arm. 'Ash Tree. The pits. Nobody's ever heard of it. The staff are all cruddy.'

'Yes, I know it,' he said.

The girl winced. 'You're not a governor, or something, are you? It's not too bad, really. Quite OK, in fact.'

'It's my wife who's a governor – of John Locke Comprehensive, where Hazel and Jill go.'

Cheryl-Ann turned on to her stomach and no longer covered her face. Some of the shyness went and she began to look friendly. He could see the resemblance to Sybil Day, though she was not as good-looking as her mother. Perhaps that would come. Could he recall seeing her around the school? It was hard to think what this near-naked girl would look like in the boxy school uniform. Put the other way about, that was why they had to wear the uniforms, of course.

He tried to study her. She could easily be the pupil who had sauntered in front of him yesterday, when he was walking to Ruth's. The long, thin legs could be right, and the compact bottom. He felt suddenly ashamed. Christ, had he really started drooling over the bodies of kids? His taste had always been for well-covered, mature women: a flesh man, as Iles had said. It came to something when a man had to be damped down by his own daughter. He should have gone in to the discussion group. Perhaps he was starting to understand that Lolita Man too well. A cop could come to resemble his quarry, the relationship was so close.

'How do you get home from school, Cheryl-Ann?' he asked.

The question seemed to offend her. The girl's face lost all its amiability and at once she became agitated and looked suspicious, as if there had been an unforgivable intrusion on some totally private section of her life, or into some secret misery. Sitting up straight, she pulled a towel around her shoulders.

He glanced at Hazel to see whether she understood what was wrong, but his daughter only shrugged and made a face. 'Questions, questions,' she said. 'What are you, the bogies or sump'n?'

In an attempt to recover ground, he said: 'I hear you're a car nut, Cheryl-Ann.' Didn't it hurt to speak that wet name? 'You're into vintage models, aren't you?'

This did not seem to work, either, and the girl sat huddled under the towel, her head hunched forward. In a little while she stood up and said: 'I'm getting cold. I think I'll dress now.'

He watched her as she walked up to the house. Yes, she could be the girl ahead of him yesterday.

'You're pop-eyed again,' Hazel snarled. 'Do you think that when you're about thirty-seven you'll have developed into a dirty old man?'

Megan's seminar ended and some of the people came into the garden drinking whisky or vodka and still buzzing with their topic. Sybil Day said: 'Even leaving aside injuries, literature is full of sex failures. Widmerpool couldn't do it with the ball-breaker, Mildred.'

'The stud in *Midnight Cowboy*,' Megan added.

'The porter,' Hazel said. 'Booze gives the desire but takes away the ability.'

'There's a thesis here,' Megan declared. 'Call it *Soft Times*.'

Sybil Day tried to help Harpur into the chat. 'It can make men violent, I believe. Even make them kill.'

He did not want to start on this, especially in the presence of children. 'I've heard that.'

Cheryl-Ann reappeared, dressed now in baggy grey trousers and a mauve, baggy shirt, but she stayed up near the house, obviously eager to leave.

Her mother sailed on: 'Isn't it a fact that rapists don't normally use much more force than they have to, but if they can't penetrate they sometimes want to destroy the victim – the only witness to the failure? That's one reason they sometimes kill. The other – where children are concerned – is that the man wants to preserve the child as child for ever. He's obsessed by innocence and thinks he can, well, seal it in, as it were, by death. The Wendy syndrome, is it called, after the girl in *Peter Pan*?'

Harpur said: 'Yes, I've heard about both those ideas.' The cheerful theorising struck him as crazy. She spoke as if the danger were far away, only a notion, like something in Lawrence or Hemingway.

'The Lolita Man can't finish? Is that why he kills?' This could be the voice he had heard through the door.

'That's possible,' Harpur told her. 'Some rapists suffer from both – the love of innocence and the inability to despoil it: a kind of involuntary reverence.'

Sybil said: 'But I thought these children had actually been raped.'

Harpur felt he had been dragooned into the discussion group after all. 'Legally it might be rape. He's not too efficient at it, so the medics advise.'

'He should write to Marje Proops,' Jill said.

IO

28 June
Today, he wasn't there. I didn't know what to do. I looked
where he always is but could not find him. Now and then I
thought I could feel him watching me from somewhere, yet I
could not find from where. Oh, why do you hide? I looked in
other streets, right up Canberra Avenue, searching, searching.

As I wrote previously, yesterday it seemed he was anxious
when our eyes met in silent contact. I should have seen then that
something was going wrong. That was the time I should have
spoken to him. It might be too late now. I cannot bear that
thought. I must look for him again and look and look.

I had to go out in the evening, bearing with me my sadness
and worry, and meet other people, some girls who were quite
kind and nice. At times I wanted to tell them of my sadness. It is
so much to bear alone. I'm afraid they would not understand,
however. They are but children. One of them is the same age as
I, but nobody has ever experienced such a relationship as mine.

Their father is police, although he doesn't look too bloody,
and he began asking a lot of questions which I didn't like. I was
trying to be nice and cheerful so nobody would know anything
was wrong, but the questions brought me back to my awful
sadness again. The questions were like he knew something
about us, yet this is not possible. He wanted to know the way I
went home from school. Why did this interest him? How could
he know that it is on my way home that I see Mr Dark Eyes? He
cannot, cannot know this. He cannot know anything about
wonderful him.

There have been other days when he wonderful he did not
come and I was not so sad as now. This time I'm sure something
is wrong, because he looked so bad the other day. Perhaps
tomorrow I'll find him again and it will be all right.

I I

It is near now. This thought calms me and I shall be able to sleep soon.

Today I saw her but did not let her see me. She was very worried, I could tell, like a frantic bird in a cage, fluttering every way, searching. I wanted to go to her then because I could see she was so sad.

But I didn't. I thought the detective, Harpur, that thick lump of piggery, could be spying and waiting. They are mostly stupid, but sometimes not. Once, when she was looking for me, she ran into Canberra Avenue and I thought maybe she was going to that house where I saw Harpur stop and pretend to do up his shoe lace that day and I wondered if she was going there for a secret meeting with him and dirty sex. You can never tell with any of them, even when they are so young and wear straw hats to school, but she did not stop. I shouldn't think these cruel things about her.

It made me cry to see how frightened she was. She does need me, it's clear now. Soon I'll go to her.

I2

Harpur found himself idling while he waited for the call from Ethan and Lane to interrogate their prisoner. He could not believe they had it right, yet the chance that they did made him sluggish about following other inquiries. The fact was that he deeply wanted next door's prisoner to be the Lolita Man, longed for an end to all the frustration and threat, so for a few minutes now and then he would let his optimism loose and assume Ethan and Lane knew what they were doing. There must be undisclosed, clinching evidence to link their man with

57

the killings. Surely to God they would have done something to stop the rumours flying, otherwise.

And then Harpur's brain would get into gear again and his doubts take the driving seat. In this limbo, while standing by for the county's message, he rang Ruth to see whether she could get to one of their hotels for the afternoon.

'Come here,' she said. 'Didn't we agree?'

'OK, but –'

'Fail not.'

To welcome him to her house now seemed strangely important to Ruth, a kind of calculated defiance of Iles, almost a regularising of their love. As she had suggested last time, he entered through the garden. His radio whistled and gossiped on her dressing table, but left them to themselves again. When it was nearly time to leave she brought him strawberries in bed.

'Barton knows, too,' he said.

'That figures. Are you bothered?'

'You were bothered.'

'Still am. I don't want to come out of this looking like a slag. And I don't want you to come out of it looking like someone who pounces on shattered widows. You're not just an opportunist, are you?'

'We've got something good going here.'

She had removed all the pictures of Avery from the bedroom. Where one of them had stood was now a vase of lilies, not his favourite flower but better than an invitation to recall what her husband had looked like washed up on the shore.

'If Barton and company know, there's no point in hoping they don't,' she said. 'I'd like you to keep them quiet, that's all. I mustn't do anything to hurt the boys. It's been bad enough losing a father.'

'OK.'

She kissed his ear. 'You're melancholy today. It's the Lolita Man business?'

Perhaps it was beginning to darken his life, as it had darkened Barton's, but he said: 'No, I don't let the job do that, ever.' Before coming here this afternoon he had been out to Spring Lane, where the body of their first girl had been found. He took the dark-haired dummy and went over yet again with their informants there the description of the suspect man seen nearby all those months ago. One of them thought they had the shirt wrong on the dummy, but couldn't say what was right for colour or style.

Harpur left the bed and went to look at the street from behind the edge of the open curtains.

'Iles out there with his bloodhounds?' she asked through a strawberry.

He watched a girl of about fourteen in the uniform of Ash Tree School approach up Canberra Avenue. She looked frantic, gazing about wildly as if searching desperately for someone, occasionally running and now and then stopping altogether to stare behind. In a moment she would hurry on again. Despite the clothes, he recognised Cheryl-Ann, who used to be Jennifer. She wore a yellow boater trimmed with school colours on her brown hair, and her long, slender legs were in grey stockings, regardless of the sun. He stared. The last time he had seen this girl in the street she had seemed happy and relaxed, idling her way home as if borne by lovely dreams. Now, she was appallingly distressed.

'Christ, what is it? You're transfixed,' Ruth said.

'Nothing.'

'You can be seen, you know. You should come away from the window.'

He turned back and dressed quickly. Good God, what was the matter with this child? Now, and the last time he had seen her, she seemed near to breakdown. What upset her? Had some boyfriend stood her up today and yesterday? Was there usually a rendezvous on the way home? She didn't look the type to have boyfriends yet. He tried to remember what it had been during the conversation in his garden yesterday that had disturbed her so much. Wasn't it simply that he had asked how she went home from school and then, in a doomed attempt to smooth things over, tried to talk to her about cars? Something had happened, or was happening now, that had turned her very sensitive. Or perhaps she was just one of those highly strung kids always liable to lose control. The thin, almost frail-looking, body would be right for that type.

He kissed Ruth and left hurriedly, hoping he might be able to meet the girl as if by accident and try again to find out what was wrong. By the time he had gone through the garden, though, Cheryl-Ann was not in sight. Perhaps she had given up and gone home. He walked to his car, parked a discreet half-mile from Ruth's house, and climbed in beside the dummy, occupying the passenger seat today.

'Like a bit of girl flesh then, do you, you black-browed bugger, even if you're not sure what to do with it when you've got it?' Harpur said. 'None of that in Parkhurst, you know. I'll still be able to admire it when you're stuck in a little barred box for thirty years. Are we OK left, partner?'

At the station there was still no invitation from next door to go and question their prisoner. Iles looked into his room, full of good humour and menace. 'Col, have you seen television news – the production those berks mounted for getting their bloke in and out of court this morning? Beautiful, beautiful, as big as *Ben Hur*. Flashing lights, blanket over the head, handcuffed to two gorillas, a convoy of vans and cars and motor cyclists. Better than the Wops did for the Red Brigade. God, are they going to look idiots when it all collapses, and, God, kindly make it collapse in full view of us, would you? We don't give them one word from our King Richard lady about the black-haired charmer in the car.' He chuckled. 'Lane will never recover from this, not even if he promised half his pay to the Church and went on a pilgrimage wearing sacks.'

'Really about the only way it could collapse, sir, is if there was another job done now.'

'You're not going fucking pious on me, are you, Harpur? You're getting a bit fond of that. If you want to bleat and weep piss off and do it somewhere else. Look, Col, would I wish the savage death of a child, I, Desmond Iles? But of course not. My only desire is to see Lane dig a pit for himself so deep that he will never get out to threaten the happy integrity of this Force.'

He nodded to himself for a while. 'By the way, I know you're up to your eyes, what with one thing and another, and all these worthy thoughts you like to indulge, so I've presumed to tell Hubert Scott to do that little task we agreed about – he'll nip down to Warwick University and see what he can unearth on Lane. I knew you'd have no objection. The point is, it could keep on slipping your mind, when you're so full of worries about girldom, as it were. I suggested Hubert might say he was from the Conservative Party, vetting Lane as a possible Parliamentary candidate. They do that sort of thing, you know. Very fussy lot, the Tories. That OK, then? This dolt, Lane, will sink himself, probably, but no reason why we shouldn't knock a few holes in the bottom, too.'

13

29 June

Again he was not there. Again I searched in vain.

Tomorrow it is Saturday and I shall be able to search all day. But where should I begin? Oh, my dear Mr Dark Eyes, why have you deserted me? Why?

14

Today I watched again without allowing her to see me, I don't understand what is happening. I'm so confused and so much in pain that I shan't sleep tonight, though I lie here in the dark and have taken a pill and drunk some Scotch.

Two terrible things happened today. Once more she went into Canberra Avenue and I thought she was looking for me, she seemed so worried. From where I was hidden I watched her run and stare about and again I nearly went to her, it was so sad. She seemed too young to be tested like this, and it may not be fair to her. But then I suddenly saw that big, thick cop, Harpur, in the house he stopped at before. He was upstairs and he was watching the street from the window. The thing was he was naked. Just standing there like some bloody flasher. That was what made me sick and makes me sick now. Anybody could see he was ready for dirty sex. I thought then what I thought yesterday that she was not looking for me at all, but she was on her way to meet him in the house. I was nearly crying, nearly shrieking my pain aloud. She didn't stop there, she didn't go in. I don't think she looked up and saw him, either. I hope not. A young girl should not have to look at things like that. Why should he be there?

Well, that thug knows about her, even if she doesn't know about him. That's why he was in the house and in the window ballock-naked, so he can look at her. He wants to get his big, heavy-duty hands on that nice, slender, gentle body. I know this, and I must protect her. As soon as she meets him and he gets his hands on her she won't be a lovely young girl any more, but just a slag. She does need me, it is obvious. She was looking for me and she knows she needs me. It must be tomorrow. If I wait it could be too late. She will not be at the school tomorrow because it is Saturday, but luckily I know her house. I will be able to find her there. It must be.

Later, something else that was terrible happened. It was so bad I thought the pain and shock of everything was making me ill, hurting my mind. When I was driving away after seeing her and also seeing him in the window I passed a parked car and . . . oh God, this is terrible, this is the start of all that dark agony again. I thought I suddenly saw myself in this car, like suddenly seeing yourself in a mirror you didn't know was there, but not a mirror. This man was sitting in an old Viva, in the passenger seat, waiting for somebody. He was wearing clothes like I wear, except the shirt. It frightened me. I thought, am I mad? This could be a delusion. I saw him just as I passed, only for a second, but it was true, it was just like me, I know it. His hair was dark, down over his forehead like mine used to be and he was my build. He wasn't moving, just waiting for the driver to come back. I wanted to stop and look at him again, but I was in traffic and had to go on, then turn back and go right around the system. When I came back he was gone, and the car. There was another car in the spot where I saw him.

I began to wonder if he had really been there and if the car had been there. Has my mind been damaged by all the things that have happened these last months? The thing is, if you have a lot of shocks the mind can go bad, and you are not in control. I had a big shock seeing that big copper staring down at her all ready for it, staring at her nice little straw hat and her dear, worried face. That was a scene out of hell. This is the kind of shock that can smash a man's mind and make him see things that are not there, like seeing yourself outside yourself.

I can't let myself go on suffering like this and maybe getting ill. Yes, I must be close to her immediately. Tomorrow. If I don't, there will be no more sleep for ever.

15

Without fully understanding why, Harpur began to grow obsessed about the safety of Cheryl-Ann Day. After all, he had simply seen the child looking distressed a few times, nothing worse than that. Yet the recollection of those moments in the street and in his garden stuck with him and were as vivid and as chilling as his mind's picture of that dead girl on the bed at the King Richard. He hardly slept. The fear he had mentioned to Garland gnawed him, and was sharper now: he could not accept that they had the Lolita Man inside next door, and while Ethan and Lane were slobbering over each other in celebration he might do his next killing. Christ, it could be here, on Harpur's doorstep, the kid of friends.

But, again, he had to ask himself why he should think so. Where was the evidence? A child seemed on edge and bothered, so he assumed she was about to be raped and murdered. Crazy. His brain and his police training must have packed up and left, and panic had moved in. He was over-heating, and he thought he might know why. This plain, gawky child had been able in some bewildering fashion to stir him sexually, and all at once he saw what might drive someone like the Lolita Man. Guilt part-explained his fixation about Cheryl-Ann, he knew that.

On Saturday morning things were so bad that he asked Megan to telephone the Days' house and find out in some roundabout way whether the girl was all right. 'You can say you're phoning to add another to the list of literary impotents – Portnoy found he couldn't do it with girls, only with pieces of liver from the fridge.'

She looked puzzled and suspicious at his sudden entry into literary games, but she must also have spotted genuine worry, so made the call. Nobody replied. 'Eric and Sybil are almost always out catering to wedding receptions at the weekends,' she said.

'Does the girl go with them?'

'I don't think so. She's old enough to stay in the house alone. Why all this concern, Col?'

'I'm not sure.'

'Is the case getting at you, love? You're re-running horrors from the past?'

'Possibly.'

'Why link Sybil's daughter to it?'

'She acts strangely, that's all. You're right – it's fanciful.'

'And the Lolita Man's inside, anyway.'

'Possibly. You say the Days are out of the house regularly on Saturdays?'

'Sybil always calls it their busiest day. What you'd expect.'

So anyone watching Cheryl-Ann might have observed that much and know she was always left behind. 'Is she their only child?'

'Yes.'

In half an hour Harpur telephoned again, not knowing or caring much what he would say if someone replied. Nobody did.

Iles expected him to stick around the house today in case they rang from the county with an invitation to ask questions. Well, stuff Iles. The ACC wanted Lane led ever deeper into the mire, and pretending to believe they had the Lolita Man locked up was supposed to help. Iles must be hoping Ethan and Lane would go the whole distance and actually charge this nobody with their two killings. Let Iles manage his own dirty tricks, organise his own career game. There were bigger things, like danger to a child for one.

Harpur took the Days' address from Megan and drove over to

64

the house. It was a big, detached, modern place with a lot of glass and well-screened by trees and privet. That might be a help. He walked up the drive and rang the bell. No cars were in sight, so Megan probably had things right, and they must be working. There was no answer.

He began to walk around the house, gazing in at each big picture window, looking for evidence of something wrong. He spotted no signs of trouble. But it was not the downstairs rooms which interested him. Somehow, he had to get inside and check the bedrooms. That picture from the King Richard was still in his head.

Jesus, it would take some explaining if they returned suddenly, or if neighbours had seen him prowling and came to investigate. Was it all stupid and fevered, anyway? Doubts swamped him again. Why didn't he simply go home and wait for the county's call, hoping for the best? Megan may have hit the button when she suggested the case was now reaching his marbles. There were times when he relied on Megan's sharpness and balance and at those times and some others he knew he was lucky to have her. Now, he felt like putting before her all the elements in his anxiety over Cheryl-Ann and asking whether they made sense: all the elements except his own flickering lust for the girl and the special interests which had taken him to Canberra Avenue and those streets near Ash Tree School. Megan was first-class on what did or did not 'make sense'. The phrase was one of her favourites. Their daughter, Jill, had picked it up.

And then, at the rear of the house, just as he had decided he was in the grip of a sick imagination and ought to leave, he found a window broken and open. It was a crude job, with almost all the glass smashed just to reach the catch, and anybody inside the house would have been alerted by the din. The messiness and amateurism made Harpur even more alarmed. This was not a burglar but someone with another reason for entering. At once he climbed in.

It was the kitchen. From the window across the tiled floor to a door stretched occasional small traces of dirt, as from someone's shoes. Again he was reminded of that room at the King Richard, and of Hubert Scott busy with his dustpan and brush while Desmond Iles purred. Now Scott was after more dirt for him, down at Warwick University. Nothing had sprouted from the soil he found earlier.

Harpur quietly crossed the big kitchen and emerged into a red-carpeted hall. Here a couple more fragments of earth had been dropped. For a second he stopped and listened, but picked up no sound. Ringing the door bell might have put anyone in the house on guard, if there was anyone still here left alive. Full of terror he began to mount the stairs, terror not because he might meet an intruder, but at the thought of finding the girl's body. On the landing he paused again and looked around. He saw on one closed door an oblong of unpainted wood, as if a name plate had recently been removed. He guessed it must have read 'Jennifer's Room' and she had not been able to replace it yet. On the sanded floor near this door was another fleck of shoe dirt. Stepping forward very carefully he put his ear against the door panelling. Again he heard nothing.

He turned the knob slowly and then, because it was habit and training and safer, he shoved the door back hard and burst in ready for almost anything, even the sight of a wrecked child. But there was nobody in the room, alive or dead. His relief at seeing the bed empty was so great that he heard himself grunt aloud, 'Thank God, thank God.' What had happened to him? Couldn't he take strain as it came any longer?

What had happened to *him* did not rate. Where was Cheryl-Ann? Where was whoever had broken in? The room was chaotic, a shambles of clothes, cups, record sleeves, books and pop papers. It might be the normal squalor of a kid's room, or had there been a struggle? Nothing seemed broken, and he saw no blood. Portuguese tourist posters hung intact on the walls. The place was grossly scented but he thought he also caught for a moment a small whiff of some especially pungent tobacco breath, as if someone who smoked French or Spanish cigarettes had been in the room recently.

Quickly he looked through the other bedrooms but still found nothing that said violence. Returning to the girl's room, he began a hurried but skilful search, trying to leave things pretty much as they had been. Girls of this age wrote love letters, didn't they, and received them? Or they did when

66

Harpur was young. Perhaps that would be regarded as soft now. All the same, there might be something here to account for Cheryl-Ann's deep anxiety and maybe provide a clue to where she was now. Possibly she kept a diary. Both of Harpur's daughters did off and on. He wanted names – of people, of places. Working systematically, he went through a couple of chests of drawers and a wardrobe, then pulled books one by one from a shelf and flicked through the pages, in case letters were hidden inside. An ottoman chest had been converted into a toy box and he rummaged through the relics of her earlier years: dolls, board games, tin tea sets. An album of snapshots contained many of her as a baby and smaller child but offered no help.

When he had finished he left the house through the shattered window, leaving it open as before. All his worries remained, and were worse now he knew the house had been broken into. His failure to understand had grown, too. If this really was the Lolita Man, there had been yet another change of style. For him to break in and look for a girl he knew would be unprotected might be in the pattern of the King Richard. But to take her away? That would be hugely difficult to manage in secrecy, if she was alive. And if she was not, what point?

His radio handset was in the Viva and he should have checked with the nick to see whether the call had come from Ethan and Lane. He had no time for that. Instead, he began to scour the streets in his car, slowly covering all the area around Ruth's house, the school and the Days' district. When the radio tried to speak to him he ignored it.

After half an hour he realised suddenly that he was expecting Cheryl-Ann to be in her school uniform, but it was a Saturday and he had seen those clothes hanging in a wardrobe. Instead, she might be wearing the baggy trousers and shirt she had on the other evening. He tried to recall whether either of those garments had been in the room, but couldn't. So, if it came to putting out a description of her, he would be unable to describe her clothes. Had the moment arrived for him to make that move: report her missing and get a drag-net operating? One man searching alone could do next to nothing. Was he wasting time?

At once he decided he still did not know nearly enough to authorise a full-scale trawl. The girl might be quite safe somewhere. He had no more evidence to say otherwise than when he had started this. A broken window showed only that somebody had entered the house.

Near a stretch of wild, open land up behind the school he left the car and began to walk a criss-cross pattern through the patches of woodland, moor and bracken. Light rain had begun to fall and few people were about. He had no topcoat and was soon drenched, but kept going. This piece of ground lay not far from the site of one of the earliest Lolita killings, a girl called Emily, at Sturt Fields. There, the body had been well concealed in a ditch and carefully covered with foliage, and a terrier had found it and barked until his master came to see what was wrong. Harpur looked now for likely hiding places, shifting fallen branches and pushing his way through dense clumps of bushes. There was something desperate about it, something frantic and irrational still. The girl killings fell into two types, as far as they knew. In the King Richard it had been quick and done at the spot where the Lolita Man cornered the child. In the other two on their ground – and probably in the two next door, though this was not totally clear – the girls had been held somewhere for up to seventy-two hours alive, then killed and dumped. None of the cases suggested the body would be found in the open so soon after disappearing. Yet he felt compelled to go on. Until today he had never believed in policing by instinct or in detection that put leaps of faith in place of logic. Something inside him must be askew.

After a couple of hours his hands and face were torn by brambles and mud streaked his clothes. He drove home. Megan and the girls were out shopping but there was a note saying Iles had telephoned three times. Harpur rang back.

'Where the fuck have you been?' Iles said before Harpur could speak.

'Something came up.'

'What came up?'

'A possible lead, sir.'

'Do I get to hear about it, perhaps? Do any of us get to hear about it?'

'It's early stages, sir. I can't say there's anything in it yet. Probably not.'

'Nice one, Col. You're supposed to be ready on call for a trip to the sodding Holy See. They've been trying to reach you. What happened to your radio?'

'On the blink, I think.'

'Oh, yes? Anyway, it's on over there. Lane wanted you to do your first interrogation this evening.'

'But it's rubbish, sir.'

'Of course it's rubbish, dear son. That's the bloody point, isn't it? We've got to help this pair of carpet-baggers towards the edge of the cliff.'

'But in the circumstances, sir, all that seems unimportant. A bit of trivial politicking.'

Iles fell briefly silent. 'We've discussed this previously, I think, Col. I know you have your point of view, and I naturally respect it. All I'd add now is that, if our Police Authority brought in someone like Mark Lane as Chief, someone with medieval Mick ideas about adultery and God knows what else, there could be all sorts of unpleasantnesses, couldn't there – disciplinary complexities where women of colleagues or former colleagues are involved, witch-hunts, marriages fucked up simply by gaff being brutally and piously blown? This is something we do not do here, at least not to date. Where would you be, or your bloody friend Garland? Believe me, Col, I've absolutely no intention of starting anything like that, I mean, dropping damaging and tactless words to a man's children, say, and upsetting them. We're grown-up here, and we look after each other. I believe this an estimable feature of our team. Lane would be something so different, and I do feel I'm entitled to seek your aid, yours especially, in preventing his coming.'

'I –'

'So get over there tomorrow and don't piss me about further, or disappear into your hot little nooky nest. Who the hell are you to get sniffy over politicking? How do you think a police force runs, for Christ's sake? Lane says it's too late now for a question session this evening. There are lawyers scuttling about the place and he doesn't want any suggestion that their prisoner is being given the twenty-four hour sleepless treatement. We had an extremely amiable chat. I think I might even call it comradely. He has some fine qualities, but unfortunately they don't stand a chance against all the others and his birth, like having one good tooth in a gobful of ruins. I've told him you will be there without fail at 2.30 p.m. tomorrow. He has to tag along to what they call it in the morning – *marss*. So sodding well be there. You know the way, do you? Grand.' Iles put the phone down.

Harpur had a bath and heard Megan and the girls come in. When he joined them Megan said: 'Sybil Day phoned.'

God. 'Yes?'

'They've had a burglar.'

'Yes?'

'He broke in through a kitchen window.'

'Yes?'

'Do you know about this? Have the police found it?'

'No, I don't think so.' Get to the child. He wanted to yell it, but let her go at her own pace.

'Well, nothing seems to have been taken, absolutely nothing. Isn't it strange? She said, should she report it, and I told her, of course she should. That's right, isn't it? There's no knowing what –'

He cracked. 'What about the girl?'

'What about her?'

'Is she all right?'

'Cheryl-Ann? Depanic yourself. She's there.'

'You're sure?'

'She's been with them at a reception all day. A waitress cried off at the last minute and their daughter had to fill in. She says someone has been through her things, but that's the only damage.'

'Did you tell Sybil about Portnoy?'

'Yes. We're all invited to lunch there tomorrow to discuss things – literature, break-ins, anything. We can swim in their pool.'

'I'll drop you off but can't stay. There's some work afoot.'

'On a Sunday?'

'We never close.'

'Which means Iles is screwing you.'

'They do screw people, ACCs.'

She let that one go past. 'Work where?'

'In the county.'

'Questioning their prize? I thought you didn't think he was the one.'

'Now I'm not so sure.'

16

30 June

I could not seek him today, as I had planned. Fate was against this.

Yet I believe he has not gone away. He has not left me. I believe something wonderful and strange occurred in my absence. I believe he wonderful he came to seek me and entered my room while I was not there. Certain articles had been moved. Moreover, I believe I could smell some strong tobacco in my room like they use in those French cigarettes. Although I hate all smoking, it was wonderful to think the odour was from his breath, though this would not be pleasant in a social gathering.

It is so lovely to think Mr Dark Eyes was in my room and that he touched things which belong to me, clothes and dolls, and that he breathed in the lovely perfume called Arpège with which the air of my room is ever rich. Despite the Arpège I could smell the tobacco.

Tomorrow I really shall be free to seek him and nothing, NOTHING, can go wrong. I know, I know I shall find him. It is as if we are so close now he has been to my room.

17

There was something wrong. I could not find her. God, where was she, and where is she? I am alone, unsleeping in that black cavern of pain again, though I thought I had escaped for ever.

She should have been in her house, but no. I found her room, and it's a tip, but I don't care. She's only a child. It's why I want her. She's not some old tidy, twisting housewife, and that's good. There are plenty of them about.

I want to know where she was yesterday when I couldn't find her in the house. I searched the streets, but still couldn't find her. All the time I thought I might see her somewhere with that ape called Harpur. Maybe he was putting those thick hands on her lovely slim body. In the afternoon I grew so nervous and angry I came home, and I'm still nervous and angry because of her. Again I have to tell myself it will be tomorrow. Will she come looking for me then? Let it be, let it be.

18

It was strange to be returning to the Days' house. Last time, Harpur had parked a long way off, then sneaked across the garden and entered like a burglar, his mind full of raw fears for Cheryl-Ann. Now, he left the car right outside and his daughters, chattering and whooping, galloped ahead up the tarmac drive, eager to see Cheryl-Ann and get snorkelling in the pool. As he and Megan followed, she said: 'You seem subdued – sort of defeated. Is Iles really giving you a hard time?'

He found it almost painful to have someone know you and read you so well. 'Just sad I can't stay for long.'

'It is work, is it?'

'What else?'

'Oh, I don't know.'

She could hit back. They had developed a kind of pact not to pry too far into each other's lives. Generally, it worked well enough, though occasionally the cease-fire would break down and there would be some sniping. They both recognised, without talking about it, that they would stick together until the children grew up.

When Sybil greeted them she said: 'My daughter isn't with you, is she?'

Harpur's alarms revived.

'With us?' Megan asked.

'She seems to have left the house very early – before anyone was up. I thought she might have gone to your place to bring you over here. Not to worry. She'll be in soon.'

They went into the big, light lounge. Hazel and Jill had made straight for the garden and now put their heads around the door. 'Where's Cheryl-Ann?' Jill asked. 'We'd like to swim.'

'Go ahead,' Sybil told them. 'Change in the little garden shed. Jennifer's snorkelling stuff is there if you're short of anything.'

Harpur noticed the use of her real name, almost a correction of Jill. 'She's out for a moment,' he told the girls. He spoke as casually as he could, on guard against himself and his panics this time. 'These light mornings – it's hard to stay in bed,' he said, to comfort Sybil.

'Jennifer usually manages it pretty well.' She poured iced tea. 'But she has lots of chums on the estate. She'll be with one of them.'

Again the formal name. It made things sound bad, yet Sybil seemed to feel no strain.

'She must have been really quiet,' she said. 'I didn't sleep deeply after the break-in.'

'Is there a boyfriend?' Megan asked.

'*Cherchez le garçon?* Not that we know of. That doesn't mean a thing, of course. They're secretive little devils, aren't they? And I suppose fourteen is fourteen, after all. Look at Juliet.

One has to think that in many countries today a girl is quite grown-up at that age.'

Even now she could theorise. When her husband joined them she said: 'No, Eric, she hadn't gone to the Harpurs'.'

He shrugged. 'It's impolite. She knows Hazel and Jill are coming.'

'Don't worry a bit,' Megan told them. 'As long as they've got the pool.'

'Her tummy will bring her back.' She laughed. 'Anyway, the Lolita Man's locked up, isn't he, thank God, even if it was the opposition who got him.'

'That's right,' Harpur replied at once. 'I'm on my way to see him now.'

'We've had several of your people here about the break-in,' Day said. 'Decent chaps.'

Again Sybil laughed. 'In a way it's unnerving, the fact he took nothing. What the hell was he doing?'

'The police seem to think there might have been two of them,' Day said.

'And both empty-handed, as far as we've been able to tell. It's bizarre,' Sybil went on.

'These people specialise,' Harpur told them. 'Some want only cash, others only jewellery or cash. If they couldn't find exactly what they're looking for they'd take nothing.' Yes, if the girl had been out, nothing else there would interest the Lolita Man.

'As a matter of fact there was some cash around,' Sybil replied.

'He must have been disturbed,' Harpur suggested.

'Or they,' Day said.

Megan walked with Harpur to his car. He gave her Lane's office number. 'Just in case.'

'Of what?'

'Just in case.'

'Where will you eat?'

'Some cell meal, I expect. A take-away.'

'So long-suffering, you people. Do we value our police enough?'

They showed Harpur straight to Lane's room. Ethan was with him. 'You boys over there think we're right up shit creek on this one, don't you, Harpur?' the Chief Constable said. 'Here for a giggle, are you, and that's about all?'

'I'm here to interrogate, sir, in the hope that we have seen the last of these monstrous crimes.'

'Hark at him,' Ethan replied. 'Who wrote those lines for you, the Moderator of the Church of Scotland or Desmond Iles?' Neat and fit-looking, in a fine grey summer suit and what might be an old boy tie from a decent school, Ethan sat sideways in an armchair, his long, elegant legs dangling. The black slip-on shoes had cost something. Occasionally, when Iles was not feeling too venomous, he used to call Ethan 'Fauntleroy', and Harpur could see why today. Handsome, with small, cheery features, the Chief Constable was almost boyish and came close to appearing sensitive, though not disastrously close. Like so many men in the highest ranks he did not look like a policeman at all but might have been an accountant or a dentist. Harpur wondered if he personally ought to try losing a bit of bulk.

'We'll nail this one eventually,' Ethan said, 'and the Lodge will be laughing on the other side of their moronic chops. This is the right guy, no question, isn't it, Mark?'

'Indeed yes, sir.'

'What else can he say?' Ethan asked.

'It's great if it's true,' Harpur said.

'Well, you put on a good face, I'll give you that,' Ethan told him. 'Tell me, how have they knocked you into shape over there? You're not part of the Craft, I hear. Who's your sponsor?' He stood up and glanced down approvingly as the suit shed its creases. 'Mark will look after you this afternoon. I'm due elsewhere. Listen: this lad's a toughie, very hard to shift. He admits nothing, though it's written all over his degenerate phiz. But I want none of your impact techniques used on these premises, you understand? What you do over there is up to you, but here we believe a man is entitled to his dignity, even a buttock freak. I've always maintained that a police force is the product of a civilised society and has a duty to act in a civilised style. If you look from the window you'll see a plashy fountain in the grounds and a few pieces of quite respectable sculpture if those sods from Traffic aren't pissing about with them again. That's the kind of image I want for my outfit, not a clenched fist with someone's front teeth stuck in it.'

'We like to get statements by skill and persistence,' Harpur stated.

'We hear the screams from here. Is it true Barton wanted to send all your CID men to on-the-job training in Jo'burg?'

When Ethan left, Lane went out with him for a moment and came back grinning. 'All balls, of course,' he said. 'No chance this is the Lolita Man. We've really tampered with him but his story never moves. He's got alibis for the dates, and they look pretty passable. Sorry to bring you over here, really, but you see what Vince is like. I have to play along. We're stuck with the charade for a little while longer.'

Lane was in shirt-sleeves and braces, without a tie. He had his shoes off and his big toes stuck through holes in both socks. He went and sat at his desk. 'But, anyway, I wanted to see you when the Chief wasn't around. Weekends he keeps for a sea captain's lady, when her husband is on business in great waters. Look, Harpur, we've got to get some sort of cooperation on this case, haven't we? It's madness as it stands.'

'How do you mean?'

'You know what I mean – the obstructiveness, the bigotry. It's a gross scandal. We've got to have a fuller exchange – one to one, you and me. Obviously, it would have to be on the quiet. Ethan wouldn't tolerate it, nor Iles. I don't know about Barton. He'll do anything for a quiet life.'

'We've got a pretty good exchange of information through the regional crime squad.'

'On basics, yes. But it's the key bits extra, the bits you pick up for yourself, or me. Can you say you're not sitting on anything?'

Jesus, this could be the hard and soft routine generally kept for villains. After Ethan did the tough, foul-mouthed turn, along came Lane, waggling his toes and showing his braces, like everybody's uncle, and applied the matey quota of homespun. Their prisoner was a dud and they knew it, so now they would try to charm out any special stuff Harpur had.

Lane said: 'Look, my Chief is – Put it this way: he really

believed we had something when we pulled in this knickers man. I thought it a possible myself. Then, as far as I was concerned, it all fell to earth very fast. Our strongest spottings are of a dark-haired guy, tanned complexion, maybe working part of his life abroad, with heavy dark eyebrows. You've probably got the same yourself.'

He waited and again Harpur wondered whether he was being pumped. 'Among others.'

Lane smiled and nodded. 'OK, I'm not asking you to put all your goodies on the table. You've got Iles to answer to, and we're the enemy. Likewise, I have to keep in step with Vince.' He shook his head slowly. 'Lord, but it's some situation. Would they believe it outside? Maybe they would. Some of them will believe anything about police.'

He sounded wearied by it and appalled, genuinely astonished it could exist. Harpur almost warmed to him. So, did that mean the performance was working?

'I think Ethan accepts now that we're not holding the Lolita Man,' Lane said, 'but going public on it is something else. There's face-saving to be done. Myself, I think the longer the worse. He insisted on that Panzer display outside the court, and he's trapped now. I've got to get him out of it without making us look total fools, and without damaging his path to the Inspectorate. All right, and without knocking my own route up, too. But the fact is, when all this weighty career stuff is out of the way, we're still going to have a bloke around pouncing on young girls. You and I ought to do something about that, so let's get together on it. Take my home number.' He gave Harpur a slip of paper. 'It will be easier to talk that way than through a switchboard.'

'I'll certainly think about this.'

Lane looked amused. 'Iles has really got you schooled, hasn't he? You can't believe any good can come out of this side. I understand. We're both organisation men. We jump when the word comes.'

'I worry about it.'

'Well, let's –'

Lane's phone rang. He answered and handed the receiver to Harpur. 'Your wife. She sounds bad.'

77

Megan said: 'Hazel took a call.'

'Where are you?'

'Still at the Days'.'

'Is the girl back?'

'No. That's the point.'

'Yes? What call?'

'A fragment. Hazel thinks it was Cheryl-Ann.'

'What did she say.'

'Cheryl-Ann was sobbing, crying. The words were not clear.'

'No, but –'

'This is two kids, Col, that's all. Try to think of it. One of them, apparently in distress, rings expecting to speak to her mother or father and gets this strange voice instead. So, everything was a jumble. Hazel says it was like a cry for help.' Her own voice seemed to tail away, as if into tears.

'What made Hazel say that?'

'Those were her words. I can't quiz her too much. She's not up to it just now.'

'Of course not. Do we know where the call came from?'

'Apparently, Cheryl-Ann didn't say. A few words, then the phone was knocked away.'

'How do we know that?'

'Hazel said she heard it crack against something, as if it was swinging on the cable. There were voices in the background, and the sound of a struggle. All the rest of us were in the garden, or Hazel wouldn't have answered. I came in because I heard her yelling down the phone. She was trying to get someone to answer while these sounds were going on behind. She realised something could be very wrong.'

Lane stood up and ambled to the window.

'She did pretty well,' Harpur said. 'Perhaps I'll be able to talk to her when she's feeling better.'

'Sybil wants to know whether she should report Cheryl-Ann missing.'

'Yes. At once. Can she give a description? Clothes? She didn't see her go, did she?'

'I don't know.'

Lane gazed out, possibly admiring the plashy fountain. Half Harpur's mind wondered whether all his calls were recorded.

'I'm going to leave now,' Harpur told Megan.

Lane returned to his desk. 'Something?'

'Possibly,' Harpur replied. This could be the first test of the new understanding between them, but if so it had come too soon. Harpur found himself still hoarding from habit.

'I'll fiddle the cell book to make it look as if you had a session with our prisoner,' Lane told him.

'What?'

'We've got to keep Ethan happy. And your people.'

Christ, even now. 'Fine. I'll be in touch.'

'I hope so.'

'I mean it.' And he did half mean it.

19

'OK, lovey, now you're coming back from the kitchen with the squash bottle and the phone rings. You pick up the receiver, the bottle in your other hand, still. You're standing here,' Harpur said. He held out the receiver, but Hazel could not bring herself to take it from him. 'You'll only hear the dialling tone, darling. Nobody there now.' But who knew what she would hear again in her head? And he wanted her to hear it again, all of it, and tell them.

To give her time to steel herself he asked, 'How long was the call, do you think, Hazel?'

'A few minutes?'

'Here we are then.' He held out the receiver again and eventually his daughter did take it and put it to her ear. Megan stood close to her. She understood what Harpur was trying to do, and seemed to understand that he had to do it, but felt the need to protect Hazel.

'Did you speak when you picked it up?' Harpur asked.

She nodded.

'Immediately?'

'I think so. I would, wouldn't I, daddy?'

'Well, I don't know. I'd like you to try to remember whether there were pips sounding when you first listened. You know – the signal that the call is coming from a public box. It goes on until the caller puts money in. That would be important for us. It would narrow things down a wee bit.'

Hazel grimaced. 'I can't remember.'

'Think, sweetheart. Look, if you spoke at once, while the pips were still sounding, you might have repeated what you said – after they'd ended. They can't hear you properly until then. Can you remember whether you had to speak twice?'

She considered this. 'I don't think so. I was just listening.'

Harpur would have plugged away at it, but saw Megan's face. Coming the heavy with your own daughter was pushing things. 'Right. So what did you say, Hazel?'

'I made a mistake, dad.' Her head slumped.

'Yes?'

'I gave our number. I forgot I was in someone else's house.'

'It's easy to do. I've often done it.' Appalled, he tried to imagine the Day child at the other end, perhaps snatching a second somehow to make the call and then hearing the unaccustomed voice and the wrong number. 'Did you realise at the time what you'd done? Did you correct?'

'I was going to. I was going to read this number.'

'Show me what happened.'

Hazel bent down to read from the dial. For a moment the receiver was away from her ear. It might have been then that Cheryl-Ann gave her location, or perhaps her own number.

'Then I heard something coming over the receiver and I listened properly again. I didn't give the number again. I don't think so.'

'That's fine. Now, you heard something and put the phone back to your ear. Can you remember exactly what it was? Words?'

She shook her head and hesitated, horror on her face. She could hear it all again. Megan put an arm around her shoulders and said: 'Take it easy, darling. It's tough, we know that, but you can see it's very important Colin should know all there is to know quickly. It might help with the search.'

They were still in the Days' house, Harpur, Megan and Hazel standing near the little, low telephone table, Sybil and Eric Day seated close together on a settee. Francis Garland was in a chair near Hazel, a tape recorder running on his lap. In another room Jill watched television.

'Not words,' Hazel replied.

'A voice, though?'

'Yes, it was the sound of a voice, a girl's. At first she was crying, a sort of sobbing.'

'Did you speak when you heard that? Did you ask who it was?'

'I might. Daddy, I can't really remember, it was all so quick. All I can remember is what I heard.' She seemed about to break down into sobbing herself. Then she said: 'I don't think I asked who it was because I thought I recognised Cheryl-Ann's voice straight away, even sobbing it sounded like her, and I knew she was out, and everyone puzzled, so it could be her ringing to say where she was.'

'Of course.'

The Days were holding hands, both sitting very stiff and forward on the settee, staring at Hazel, as if trying to help her and will her into remembering something useful, and in time.

'Then the sound went sort of weak. It was still there, but like what happens when someone turns their head away for a moment when they're phoning. She was talking, but I couldn't hear what she said.'

These could have been more seconds when Cheryl-Ann gave something they needed to know. She might have been looking behind, in case he had spotted her at the phone and was rushing to stop the call.

'I think I spoke to her then. I said, "Cheryl-Ann, where are you?" I think I said people here were a bit worried. I think I said, "There's a bit of a panic going on about you, Cheryl-Ann." I said it like that, just a bit of a panic, because I didn't want to upset her, because she was already upset if she was sobbing. Well, I didn't know what to say, really. I was afraid something pretty bad was going on.'

At least the girl would have known by then she was speaking to the right number. 'And did she answer?'

'She said, "He's coming now, he's seen me."'

Sybil Day bent her head forward, perhaps to hide tears.

As if unnerved by the tension, Hazel said: 'It could be the other way about, "He's seen me, he's coming."' What did it matter? Hazel simply needed to say something, anything, to relieve her stress. 'I think Cheryl-Ann was afraid then,' she added after a while.

'Did you ask who was coming?'

'Oh, yes.'

The door bell rang and Garland put the tape recorder on the carpet, still running, and went to answer. In a little while he came back with Desmond Iles, who made a small, self-effacing gesture to Harpur, an apology for interrupting. The ACC looked stricken by sadness and nodded in sympathy to Eric Day. Garland sat down again, leaving the recorder on the floor.

'You asked her who was coming,' Harpur prompted.

'Daddy, I'm getting tired. Do I have to go on standing here, holding the phone? It doesn't help me remember anything.'

Iles hurried to bring a dining chair for her. 'I know you're doing wonderfully,' he said. Hazel and Jill both liked Iles, found him what they called 'hilarious' and 'fun'. It was one way of thinking about the ACC, a way available only to those who did not have to take his orders. Hazel smiled now and seemed reassured.

Sitting down, she put the receiver back on its cradle. 'Cheryl-Ann said, "He's coming from the car," and then she said, "Oh, he's so different, it's so different." Then she started to cry again and –'

Once more Hazel stopped. Nobody spoke or moved. The tape recorder purred.

'Then she did scream.'

Day gave a short groan. Iles, who was standing behind the two of them, now leaned forward and touched Day's arm gently in consolation.

'A very short scream,' Hazel said.

'And was there any other sound behind it?' Harpur asked. He meant a male voice, or the squeak of a door being pulled open, if it was a public box, and perhaps traffic noise increasing.

'Another sound?'

'Anything.' He could not plant one of the possibles in her head.

'No. Then she sort of whispered. "Please, please, come for me, somebody come for me." She said please twice, I know that.' Again she fell silent and again the only sound in the room was the recorder turning. He watched Hazel fight to order her recollections. 'I think she had her mouth right against the receiver, and it was hard to hear the words properly, but she seemed to say something about a hill, perhaps "on a hill". Then she said, "Please" again and "Find me. Tell my dad." And then she said something I couldn't understand, it was like, "It's not the right man." And I think I said, "Who do you mean?" and I said, "Say where you are, Cheryl-Ann. Which hill? Read the number of the phone." But all she said was something else I didn't understand, I'm not sure if I heard it right. What I thought she said was, "Mr Dark Eyes is him, he's not like what I thought." That was all.'

'Mr Dark Eyes?' Those reports from the earliest attack could have it right, then.

'Yes.'

'Did you know what she meant?'

'No.'

'It sounds as if she thought you'd understand. Did she talk about somebody when she was over at our house the other day?'

'No.'

'You're sure?'

'I'd remember something like that, dad. She didn't talk much at all. You know that.'

He turned to the Days: 'I wonder if this means anything to you? Mr Dark Eyes. Is there a boy or man around who would fit? Someone with a car?'

Eric Day shook his head. 'I think Sybil has already told you this: we don't know of any boy at all. Jennifer never seemed like that.' He sounded almost angry, as if the child had been slurred.

'You can see it's important. If you could really try to think – anyone at all. Delivery people, for instance. Postman? Grocer? Laundry? Dustman?'

'Well, we'll think,' he replied, still offended. 'The dustman? My God.'

Hazel said: 'And then the last sound, a crash or a bump as if she had dropped the receiver and it had hit something, swinging on the wire.'

Or as if it had been pulled from her hand and used as a club.

'Then no more speaking,' Hazel said.

'But the receiver was not put back at the other end?'

'No, I could hear things going on.'

He decided not to ask what they were. Megan had already given him an account, and the Days could be spared that. 'Did you hear a car starting?'

'No. I called and called, trying to bring her back to the phone. Then mummy came in from the garden and there was nothing.'

'Nothing at first, then the unobtainable tone,' Megan said. 'I called you immediately afterwards, Colin.'

If she had not used this phone they might have still been connected and the box traceable.

'That was a super piece of memory work, Hazel,' Iles declared. He turned to Sybil: 'Colin's daughter really has given us great help here. I think we have an excellent chance of finding her now. We're going to do everything, everything. Try to be strong. I know you will.'

Megan and the children collected their swimming gear and went home by taxi. It was almost dark. Iles beckoned Harpur and Garland into the garden: 'This is desperately sad. Their daughter's a delight, as I understand it. One feels almost paralysed by grief, but that has to be conquered somehow. Time is so crucial. We'll get an Incident Room set up at once, of course. We can only guess which bloody method he's on this time. The child could be dead, or incarcerated somewhere. I fear the former, but we must believe the latter. Must. That might give us three days to find her, three days at the very most – from dawn today.'

'We don't know it was a phone box, but will have to assume so, I think,' Harpur said. 'We want a box on a hill somewhere. She couldn't give the number or read a location label in the box, apparently, although it was broad daylight, so we might be looking for a booth that has been stripped. It could be rural or a quiet suburb: Hazel doesn't seem to have heard any traffic. Possibly he yanked the receiver out after the call, if Megan got an unobtainable – so a box on a hill where there are few vehicles, no location label or number and maybe no receiver now, or a disconnected one. Or he may have hit her with the receiver and damaged it. There could be blood or hair on it. We'll get some people touring at once looking for that sort of booth. Sybil thinks she knows what the girl is wearing and we've put out a description. We'll talk to people living near likely pay phones. There could have been a row, a disturbance. And there ought to be a car, possibly a big, blue car, and a man with dark eyes.'

Iles nodded. 'Not bad at all. Look, Colin, we'd be best keeping all this to ourselves, at this stage. Get someone reliable to handle the tour of the boxes personally, with a hand-picked team. Hubert Scott could do it. I think he's back from the Warwick University trip. I feel it would be wrong to bring in the regional crime squad people on this yet. In due course, certainly, but it would be a mistake to let any of our newest material find its way to next door – at this point. Yes, I think so, sincerely. This needs very delicate handling.'

'Well, sir, I don't know,' Harpur said. 'The phone she was using could easily be on their ground.'

'It could be any fucking where at all,' Iles replied.

'Not if it was a booth, sir,' Garland said. 'Hazel thought the call lasted a few minutes. If it had been long-distance she would probably have had to put another coin in, even at Sunday's cheap rate.'

Iles considered this. 'Yes, Hazel did excellently, excellently. But we can't totally rely on her estimate of time, can we? A great deal can be said in a few minutes. This would be a very shocked youngster – understandably shocked – with things happening at a rapid rate. And then I thought I understood Colin to say we didn't know that it was a public telephone. Correct me if I'm wrong, I'm sure you will, Francis, I was late arriving. But it does appear that at this stage – and I emphasise at this stage – we have all sorts of imponderables. This is what I meant when I said it required very delicate handling. After all, this is the daughter of friends, virtually of colleagues, is it not? They are part of the team, and I for one set supreme value by the team loyalties in this Force. I'm not ashamed of this: the contrary.

'Have you thought that the poor wee creature may have been

naked in this box, injured, having broken from the attacker? Just at this juncture I really do not want heavies like Ethan and Lane trampling about where so many tender susceptibilities are involved. Again, this girl could be a prisoner, subject to multiple degradations. Is this the kind of situation to be invaded by some foul-mouthed shag-happy dandy like Ethan, or a Mikado bit-part tenor such as Lane? The flowers that bloom in the spring, tra-la, have fuck-all to do with this case.

'You see my point? Obviously, we'll have to put them in the picture eventually. It's only a question of judgement and timing. So, set these various things in motion now, would you, Col? Get hold of Hubert and he'll be able to suggest a couple of other tight-lipped lads. The truth is that we've nothing really concrete and reliable, have we? In a sense it would be irresponsible to offer any of it to the Papal State in its present rough form.'

Garland handed Harpur the Hazel tape.

'Anything come of Scott's excursion for background on Lane, sir?' Harpur asked.

Iles seemed to ignore this. Perhaps Scott had produced nothing. Then the ACC said: 'It's not important now, is it? This is a terrible thing, obviously – the Days' daughter. But, if it had to happen, this is the best possible time for us. That quaint couple next door have someone they swear is the Lolita Man in a cell and, meanwhile, who pops up? Why, none other than the said Lolita Man, going about his foul business just as before. You've been over there and actually talked to their prize, haven't you, Col?'

'Yes.'

'But total crap?'

'Yes.'

'These are certainly not circumstances in which one can laugh,' Iles remarked, 'but have you ever seen such a champion pair of twats so deliciously dropping themselves in it? What a tragedy they hadn't already charged him. Never mind. This is going to mess up Mr Lane for at least a decade. It's like that reporter who found Martin Bormann. I love it, I love it, save, of course, that the life of another child may have been sacrificed to make the point. How was he?'

'Lane? Affable.'

'That's him all right. Undoubted charm and *bonhomie*. But let's see if he's still smiling through when this bucket of slops hits him right in the kisser.'

As they were leaving, Barton arrived, eager to see the Days and offer his sympathy. 'What hope can I give them, Colin?' he asked, his voice shaking a little. Suddenly, he was sounding very old, though he looked as light on his feet and compact as ever.

'I think the girl must have seen the man before and has mentioned him to someone. She spoke of him to my daughter as if he were known about. We have to discover whom she told.'

'She may have written something down about him,' Barton suggested. 'Girls are like that.'

'Yes, that did occur to me, sir,' Harpur replied, though he could not disclose that he had already searched for letters or a journal.

'It should be a doddle now, sir,' Iles said. 'We'll have this wrapped up, and without aid from the genuflectors.'

'I don't care where the help comes from, Desmond. Do you hear? This child – she must be saved, if it's at all possible. Don't forget Ethan and Lane have broken bread with us, taken our salt, sung at our piano. They are not all rottenness. My God, how could I go content into retirement if we missed on this girl? I think I've met her with the Days. Lively kid.'

'Exactly, sir. I've been saying we have a special duty,' Iles replied. 'It is ours, specifically ours, and we know how to respond. I'm glad you agree, sir.'

From home Harpur telephoned Lane and told him that the Lolita Man might be in business again. He gave him Cheryl-Ann's description and everything he knew or guessed at or hoped about the telephone call to Hazel, and the big blue car, and the man with dark eyes. 'It may not be a pay phone at all. My daughter says the girl was speaking with her mouth close to the receiver at one stage, and that could mean she didn't want to be overheard by someone inside a house or building, I suppose. It's a gamble. Not one for the regional crime boys yet, though, or it will get back to Iles and he'll wonder how you heard.'

'Understood.'

'We've got to be fast.'

'I'll have something under way immediately. Thanks, Colin. This will be a two-way arrangement. I'll have things for you, I promise.'

Maybe he would, maybe not. It might all have been a sharp and successful con by Ethan and Lane. Perhaps Lane knew most of it already, anyway, if his office calls were taped. Harpur could not care too much about that. There was a chance of saving the life, though possibly not the body, of this child. So, up Iles. And it would have been the same for any child, or for anyone at all. The fact that he knew the girl and had suffered a tiny tremor for her did not count. He was almost sure of that.

Afterwards he played over the tape of the conversation between her and Hazel. Some of the things Cheryl-Ann had said were a mystery, possibly explained in the moments of the call when Hazel could not hear properly. 'Oh, he's so different, it's so different.' 'He's not like what I thought.' So, there had been a period before today when she had known him and thought about him and imagined him to be other than what she found now? No, it might be pushing things to say she had known him. Possibly she had seen him about, though, and in her head decided what he was like. Kids did that, and not only kids. She might be full of romantic dreams. Hadn't she been reading one of those loud Brontë books for an exam? Who could tell: maybe the Lolita Man appeared loving and lovable, full of glamour and fine passion, with his big car? Some of the descriptions suggested a smouldering-looking youngster in stylish clothes. The dummy maker had caught that quality well. Her fretfulness in the street and in Harpur's garden might have come from a fear that she had lost him, lost someone she valued. And now the poor doomed kid had found he was not what he had seemed, after all. That's how it generally was between men and women, women and men. 'He's not like what I thought.' Yes, you could say that. It came back to the question, who had known what she thought? Had she told someone? Had she written down her view on him somewhere, and did she think these would have been found? Why did she feel the need to make a correction?

And then there was 'it's so different'. What did she mean? What was the 'it'? He ran the tape back over this stretch. 'He's coming from the car. Oh, he's so different, it's so different.' The car? Different from what? Had she seen him in another vehicle before this? Was that the big blue one, or some other? If there had been a change of vehicle they might be totally at sea, here and in the county. Christ. So much depended on Hazel's memory. Iles was probably right to be sceptical. The ACC often was right. Occasionally he got something very big wrong, that was his only trouble.

The tape contained a couple of other obscure sentences, but he thought he might understand these. 'It's not the right man,' she had said, and 'Mr Dark Eyes is him.' Who was not the right man? Had Cheryl-Ann read the press reports and seen the television coverage of the arrest next door and picked up the rumours that this was the Lolita Man? When she telephoned, she already knew this could not be so because he was with her. She could have told Ethan he had it wrong. Too late she knew the identity of the Lolita Man: 'Mr Dark Eyes is him.' That was where the childish romanticising and reality met. He played the tape right through three times all told. The more he listened to it the less he understood how he could have hesitated even for as long as he did before telling Lane and getting the search going there, too.

20

Near midnight Harpur drove to headquarters and in the new Incident Room watched and listened as search units trawled for the girl. Barton was there, standing before a map of their whole patch.

'Desmond Iles wanted to instal a blackboard and show the number of hours left to us, changing downwards all the time, like bloody bookies do with odds,' the Chief said. 'But we're dealing with a child's life.'

'Everyone's pretty conscious of the time pressure, sir.'

'Not that we're sure of it, anyway. It could all be over already, couldn't it? God.'

But they had to act as if she was still alive and a prisoner somewhere, so the main targets were abandoned warehouses, factories and tenements in the towns, and farm outbuildings elsewhere. Garland was with Hubert Scott and a few others looking at telephone booths. The Incident Room had a bustle and tenseness about it which still suggested hope.

Barton was dressed in a gold and crimson track suit, his grey hair slicked back after a shower. It was his habit when working late to take half an hour to jog around the park perimeter – what he called 'restoring the blood flow'. His wife must have picked the track suit. He looked like one of those brochure pictures about exercise for the over-fifties, the glory of the outfit meant to make up for what time had done to the body.

The Chief took a piece of paper from a tray. 'We have a description of someone hanging about the Days' house on the morning of the break-in. It clashes with every possible we've had for the Lolita Man, and especially the dark-haired charmer. This one sounds like a fair-haired Rocky Marciano.'

Harpur took the note and read a passable description of himself. 'Thuggish-looking'? 'Threatening'? Fair enough, probably. 'I think we must discount this, sir, and concentrate on the top likelihood.'

'Oh, agreed. Who knows the break-in is connected with the disappearance, anyway? Totally untypical.' He turned away from the map and looked at his watch. 'So how many hours would you say are left? Maybe Desmond's idea of the board is not so bad, after all.'

'We think she went at around 6 a.m. Sunday, sir. It's almost 1 a.m. Monday now. That's nineteen hours gone.'

'Fifty-three to go, supposing we really can allow seventy-two to start.'

'Give or take.'

'We've wasted so much time already.' He switched back to the map abruptly, as if the secret lay somewhere there, and talk was a distraction. He moved so sharply that a spray of water drops flew from his hair and rattled on the map. 'We must search the Days' house, of course. I'd like someone considerate to do that, and definitely not Typhoon Scarth who usually seems to cop these jobs. Do you think you could handle it personally, Colin? I know we had people there after the break-in, but this is different now. I still have it in mind that girls of that age get letters, write letters they don't send, keep passionate journals.'

And the thuggish-looking, threatening snoop still had it in mind that nothing of this sort would be discovered there. He said: 'A good idea, sir.'

'I'd be the last to say anything rough or malevolent about the child, Colin, but she seems to have convinced her parents that she hadn't woken up to sex yet – still getting her kicks out of *Tom and Jerry* and the occasional glass of Pepsi. Christ, some kids of fourteen are full-blown women, if you'll pardon the phrase: taken more traffic than starlets. Did you ever see her?'

'Yes, they came to the house.'

'Not pretty, maybe, but legs all the way up to her arse. Did you notice?'

'No, sir, I can't say I did.'

'Well, I'm sorry to have spoken like that. But you see what I mean? Who knows where legs like that might have taken her? So there could be some sort of secret record there, or possibly at her school.'

Harpur had been wondering about the school. 'I'll look into both, sir.'

Barton left the map again and took Harpur's arm to draw him closer. 'Desmond's well-intentioned and a fine team man, in many ways an admirable Assistant. On this one, though, he may not be altogether single-minded. Well, there's the Lodge, as you know. He goes deep into things when he goes – total loyalty, that's Des, a wholly creditable thing, but I can't get worked up to the same pitch myself. And then, of course, he's got this King Billy business. Some of his folks come from up the Malone Road in super-Prot Belfast. All told, as much as you can, keep the rabid bugger out of it, will you? Within reason, of course.'

'I'm trying.'

He nodded. 'All my soundings say he could be on a loser, incidentally. There's a big lobby for Lane to come in here after me, regardless of this case. People on the Authority are worried about Lodge domination here. There's been all this malicious press stuff about Masonry, so it's only what you'd expect from some of these ciphers. And Iles's hard line makes things no easier, I'm afraid. He's helped polarise matters. It's so unnecessary. I've known any number of decent RCs, as a matter of fact. I mean, I wouldn't go on holiday with them or let them see how much was in my wallet, but I greatly liked the way those two came over to the piano and sang at midsummer. It showed generosity of mind.'

'Lane has a great voice.'

'There are unpleasant aspects to both of them, Ethan and Lane, I don't deny that. Have you seen the bag Ethan knocks off at weekends after checking Lloyd's Register? Well, where would somebody like Vincent pick up taste? One mustn't be hard on them.' The Chief looked at his watch. The ramblings were perhaps meant to keep his mind off Cheryl-Ann's situation. Once more he stared at the map.

Harpur left and went up towards Ash Tree School. He wanted to try on himself the kind of recall exercise he had given Hazel, and would walk again the route from the school to Canberra Avenue, where Ruth lived. In the middle of the night he would see no children and no waiting parents, so as a re-run it fell badly short, but there just might be something to give his memory a prod, and he could not wait for daylight and school hours.

It seemed almost certain now that the Lolita Man had watched her from somewhere near here, perhaps even met her and talked to her. Christ, Harpur had been standing around staring and cataloguing while somewhere very near the Lolita Man was methodically setting himself up for the next spasm. Once or twice in his career before this Harpur had been forced to regard himself as useless in fighting an evil, but never as strongly as now. None of those car numbers or physical descriptions so carefully noted near the school led anywhere. But, suppose the Lolita Man had done the reasonably crafty thing and posted himself a little distance away on her route home, realising the dangers if he were too obvious. Harpur would have missed him.

Why had she looked so frantic that day in Canberra Avenue? Had he failed to turn up? There had been at least one occasion earlier when Harpur had walked in that direction – on his way to Ruth's house for that first, unexpected visit. Perhaps he had looked at the Lolita Man then, and the Lolita Man's car, without registering anything, and if he covered that ground again tonight a recollection, even half a recollection, might flicker. He couldn't let himself believe his mind had become a total dead loss.

Walking slowly, he paused at junctions and gazed right and left up side streets, striving to recall whether he had noticed the big blue car parked, probably with a man looking like the dummy in it. What kind of job would the Lolita Man have if he was free to stalk a schoolgirl in the mid-afternoon? There had been the suggestion that he might do spells overseas and return on long leaves. Or, he was possibly on shifts. He might be simply rich and idle, able to indulge his little whims. More probably he would be out of work, and that could mean the big blue car was ancient and dilapidated, say an old Humber or Rover or Mercedes or Jag that drank fuel and sold for a song. Any of these would be reasonably distinctive, but he could recall nothing like that.

Now and then he thought he might understand what she had meant in the telephone call by 'it's so different', apparently about the car. So many indicators said this child was a dreamer, a romancer. If she had been making up glamorous notions about the man, she might also have decided to do the same for his car. A girl would not want to admit that her dream man had a dream boat that was a load of rotting tin. Had she been fantasising about his car somewhere and trying to correct that in her chaotic, rushed conversation with Hazel? This still left the question of why she had needed to correct. Whom had she told about this man and his wheels?

He walked the length of Canberra Avenue then went back, as he had on that first afternoon. Conceivably the Lolita Man had worked on foot. Could he recall the dark, predatory-looking figure of the descriptions hanging about and eyeing talent? Wouldn't Harpur have noticed someone like that?

It had been during his return down the avenue that Ruth had appeared at the door and called him in. Nothing comparable happened tonight, though. He did pause, hoping she might be awake, hear his loitering footsteps and come to the window. On that earlier occasion he had pretended to do up a shoe lace, hadn't he, so there would be a chance to talk, and while he was crouched down she had invited him. Tonight he walked on. There would be no bonus, no rendezvous with Ruth. Good God, how could he think about that, anyway? He had a child to find, against the clock.

And then, as he walked, and dwelt on the distant pleasure of that first welcome to her home, something did come back, a fragment, a far-out possibility, but a possibility. He recalled that as he bent over his shoe he had missed what she said because a passing car drowned her words. Hadn't that vehicle made an exceptional din? When he thought about it now, he seemed to hear the car labouring along like a ruined tank. That noise seemed precise in his head, but he had no picture of the vehicle, even though he bullied his memory. Probably, he had not even glanced towards the car as he fiddled with his lace, intent on looking at Ruth in her doorway, and trying to catch her words. The racket might suggest not just a clapped-out big engine but something with a hole in the exhaust and pricey trouble not far off. Had he looked up would he have seen a large, blue, last-legs Rover or Mercedes or Princess or Jag or Humber, with one man in it, dark-haired and dark-eyed?

Ash Tree was not the kind of school where mummies arrived for their kids driving wrecks. Most of the vehicles were high-quality little jobs, several with personalised number plates, to make up for the anonymity of father's larger, company car. It had to be feasible that the wreck which had passed him in Canberra Avenue was the one he wanted. And Ruth would have been looking towards the street as she spoke and might have seen it properly.

He turned at once and went back to her house. A curtain twitched in a dark downstairs room on the opposite side of the avenue, so his footsteps must have aroused someone, or possibly this observer never slept, kept a continuous watch. He made his way to the back of Ruth's house and let himself in with his key. When he entered her bedroom she did not stir and he sat on the bed and gently shook her by the shoulder, switching a lamp on so she would see who it was at once and not cry out and wake her children.

As she came to she opened an eye and said peevishly: 'Why are you dressed?'

'There's something I must ask you. It's urgent.'

'The answer is yes.'

He took his clothes off and got into bed, hanging his radio on a chair again. The Avery pictures were back in position, he noticed, so he put the lights out quickly.

'Ask me what?' she muttered.

'Later.'

'Right you are. How right you are.' Later she said: 'Is it later?'

He told her about Cheryl-Ann and about the car in the avenue. She lay on her side, curled up towards him. 'Ruth, love, don't go back to sleep.'

'I'm thinking, putting my mind on re-wind.' Finally she said: 'Yes, could be.'

'What?'

'A blue car.'

'Big?'

'What's big? Could be a Princess or maybe an old Merc.'

'That would do.'

'There was something wrong with the exhaust – trailing the ground, I think.'

'Good. Driver?'

'I think a man. But I must have been looking at the exhaust because of the noise.'

'What sort of man?'

'I told you, I wasn't looking at him.'

'Sure?'

'You're beginning to shout. These walls are only lath and plaster. We'll have visitors.'

'Sure?' he whispered.

'I've got no picture of him in my head.'

He knew that void, useless feeling; had suffered it himself, and seen it in Hazel. So much of this case was about trying to resurrect what the eye might have seen or the ear heard without realising it.

Ruth began to weep quietly. It was as if thinking about her children in the other bedrooms had turned her mind towards the missing girl. 'Oh, Jesus, why can't I help? Why can't I remember? This whole sex thing, Colin – sometimes it's so sweet, sometimes so savage.'

He held her to him. 'Mostly sweet. Don't fret. This car might have nothing to do with it at all. Probably not. A car in the street, that's all. It could have been anyone's. You've helped. A Princess or a Mercedes – we can work on that.'

'It's only a guess. I mean, a Princess and a Mercedes don't even look alike.'

'We don't turn up our noses at anything. There isn't time to wait for the perfect.'

She seemed to slip into sleep and he dozed himself. When he awoke it was daylight and he realised she had been speaking to him. 'What? What time is it?' he asked.

'Only six o'clock. It's all right.'

That left forty-eight hours. He began to dress.

'What do you do now?' she asked.

'I don't know. I have to hope they've found something in the night, here or next door. I may have missed that on the radio while I slept.'

Not far from her house a patrol car drew up alongside him, the crew about to start asking questions. When they recognised Harpur the sergeant said: 'This a likely area, then, sir? You know it pretty well, don't you?'

'No, not especially. Anywhere's a likely area. I'm looking all over.'

The sergeant leaned out and brushed a pillow feather from Harpur's sleeve. 'Yes, sir. Still no leads at all.' He sounded crushed, but then forced himself to recover, perhaps because he wanted to put on a show for a senior man, perhaps because he genuinely thought things could come right. 'It's not the end yet, is it, sir?'

'Of course it bloody isn't.'

At home he made breakfast for himself and the family. When they came down, Megan said sympathetically: 'Another all-night job, Colin?'

'Time's so short.'

'Poor duck. Why don't you get a couple of hours while the house is quiet? I'll be out all day.'

'I didn't know.'

'Cheap train do to London. Shopping.'

Jill seemed to want to change this subject. 'I suppose you get cups of tea and that sort of thing if you have to stay up, dad?'

'Police know how to look after themselves, don't worry,' Hazel told her. 'It's called living off the land.'

'But all the time you're thinking of how to save her, aren't you?' Jill asked.

'Sure.'

Hazel said: 'She might have spoken the car number in that little time I took the phone from my ear. Have you considered that?'

'It's hardly likely.'

'She may think you've traced him through the computer and are right on their tail. She could be waiting for you to turn up at any minute.' Hazel seemed about to cry again.

'And any minute we will, don't worry. We're scouring everywhere.'

'And a helicopter,' Jill said. 'It's on TV.'

21

Barton had given way. When Harpur arrived at the Incident Room after breakfast the blackboard was in place and showed a possible forty-six hours left. The atmosphere there had changed. It was still tense, even frenzied, but no longer hopeful. Although people worked urgently with print-outs and cards he sensed they regarded it only as a show now. Most of them must think Cheryl-Ann dead.

Both the Chief and Iles were in front of the search map, Barton looking as if he had not slept, though he had changed from his jogging suit and wore uniform for some function later in the morning.

'Christ, the Press,' he snarled, not turning his head from the map. 'Do they know what caring is, do they know the meaning of compassion?'

'If you can't charge it to expenses, they don't,' Iles replied.

Barton went on, 'A London reporter was here before 8 a.m. asking to see me, suggesting that animosity between us and next door is preventing a proper search for the girl – all the old Lodge and Papal State stuff, Colin.'

'I'd say you dealt admirably with her, sir,' Iles said. 'Frank, honest, constructive.'

'I take no credit. Why not be frank? We have absolutely nothing to hide, for God's sake,' the Chief replied. 'We're working together, urgently, unstintingly, caringly, to save this poor girl, and others in the future. Who would undermine such effective work with measly rivalry?'

'I think she was satisfied, sir.'

'Good Lord, we need the help of the Press now. They can do so much by circulating descriptions. Why do they always want to look for muck?'

'Some of them are bred to it,' Iles answered. 'Shit smells like Costa Rica super-blend to them, I'm afraid.'

'Now, Desmond, you're sometimes vigorous in your hostility to Vince Ethan and Lane. Naturally, I understand your point of view, but can you assure me there is nothing of that kind associated with this case? That really would be most grave. It could come to an inquiry, couldn't it? Home Office farts all over the place flourishing their initialled brief-cases and impertinence. This Fleet Street bitch, with her questions and little yellow teeth – she seemed so damn sure of herself. I don't like it.'

'There was some glibness there, yes, sir. They can get a postgraduate diploma in that. But I'll certainly give you an undertaking that no rankling competitiveness or bigotry will affect my commitment in this instance or any other. I hope it hardly needs saying, sir.'

Barton grunted. 'If she hits the front page with that tomorrow, where are we – especially if we haven't found the girl by then? Or if we have, but not alive. Jesus, they'll all be at us – Parliament, those fucking bishops of all creeds, the Civil Liberties cabal, the WVS, Schoolchildren Against the Police. I shouldn't have to worry about such things when a girl is in peril.'

'I'll make a friendly and diplomatic approach to her editor, sir,' Iles promised, 'and scare the bloody balls off him. Fortunately, I've a former colleague in the Met who keeps ripe dossiers on most of those bastards. They can be leaned on. Half of them like Cub scouts and half the other half snort.'

Barton moved towards the stairs and his room. 'It's all so gratuitous, so malevolent.'

'I'll try to prevent it happening, sir.' When the Chief had gone, Iles said quietly: 'It distresses me to see him suffering. In a way, he's too fine for this job, Col. There's true nobility in him, a rich grandeur. Of course, that will go unrecognised by those above, and someone like Ethan will pick up the honours. Arise, briefly, out of your dung-heap, Sir Vincent Ethan. Incidentally, Harpur, it looks to me as if there's been a fucking leak from here to next door.'

'Oh?'

'Don't come that with me, you two-timing bastard. Have you been mouthing? I've got a voice inside that outfit and he tells me Lane was tipped off and tipped off good and early about the call from Cheryl-Ann. They've been searching telephone boxes.'

'We can tell the Fleet Street woman that, then. It proves cooperation. Should keep her quiet.'

Iles paused and nodded slowly. 'As ever, there's a great deal in what you say, Col. One has to take account of the legitimate interests of the Press, clearly. It is, after all, a crucial part of the social apparatus.'

'Many say so, sir.' To make sense of Iles you had to understand that he yearned to be responsible and good, and to sound responsible and good. He had taken pains to learn all the right thoughts and had them word perfect. The trouble was that a kind of ravenous selfishness would now and then slink up on its belly and rip the throat out of this intention. Nobody knew when it would happen, and especially not Iles. Megan, or one of her discussion group, said he was like a Miracle Play version of the fallibility of Man.

'Some fine people in the Fourth Estate and a brilliant tradition,' the ACC said. 'Think of Stanley, Woodward and Bernstein, James Cameron. Many of these people are true guardians of what is best. We should salute them.'

'Churchill himself was a journalist.'

'Yes, well sod them all, I say, bloody pompous, mischievous scribblers. They can keep their little inky fingers out of things they don't understand. And people like you or bloody Garland or whoever it was coughed a bibful to the Papes had better watch your backs. Oh, I know it's no criminal offence to be having it off with a late colleague's widow when you're supposed to be working – not a Scrubs matter. But biog details like that will do your future prospects little good, will they, when disclosed? Who wants a chief officer who goes about knocking up the women of his men, and tarnishing the image of a dead hero in the minds of his sons by popping into his bed? And someone like Garland – intruding on the decent marriage of an ACC. Do you think that will bring him accolades and promotion?'

'I'd like to get on with trying to find this child now, sir.'

Iles began to shout and people in the Incident Room looked up briefly, until they saw it was only the ACC. 'Oh, pardon me, do. Duty above all, isn't it, except when you're climbing on for a quota of the other, which seems mostly.' He moderated his voice. 'As to duty, have you spread some truths about Lane with the Rev. Anstruther, as agreed?'

'I have it in mind, sir. I was waiting to see what Scott found at the university.'

'Oh, were you? You were hoping the whole damn thing would go away, if you ask me.'

'Did Scott find anything, sir?'

'Did he really look?' He glanced at the blackboard. 'You're going to the girl's school, I hear.'

'After the Days' home.'

'The Chief is typically wise to ask you to search the Days' place personally. You know how to be gentle and considerate,

Col. Those are precious assets in an officer, especially a senior officer. The Days have appalling thoughts to dwell on. Their baby – what might be happening to her, even as we speak? Those two people live with that fear continuously since the girl went. My God, it doesn't bear imagining. I envy you the school visit. I love the smell of girls' schools, decent-class girls' schools – all that shampooed hair and the shining knees, the recitations of 'Break, Break, Break', and notes from parents explaining lateness. Some of my relatives were teachers in very reputable girls' schools.'

At the Days' house again, Harpur felt himself slipping towards something like panic. Continually now he seems to be retreading old ground and finding nothing of use. With Eric Day accompanying him he went methodically through every-thing in the house and garden and around the pool, concentrat-ing once more on the girl's bedroom, but still without any result. The waste of time chilled him.

'We've done it all ourselves,' Day said. 'In one way, I have to say I'm glad we found nothing – no love letters, no secret journal. It shows we know our daughter. Simply, a transparent child. Her life was – is, I mean is – totally open.' The stumble unnerved him for a moment, poor, starchy bugger. Harpur saw he wanted to say something else but couldn't. Then, in a little while, he found a way. Day went to his car in the drive and came back with a box from the boot, which he gave Harpur. 'Hazel left her swimming mask in the shed. It must have been the stress of – everything.' Then he hurried to his real point. 'Has Hazel by chance remembered anything else from the call?'

Day wanted to know that Harpur was still trying to coax and badger more out of his daughter's memory, but could not put it so bluntly. 'She's doing her best,' Harpur told him.

'Oh, she was splendid. I really mean it. We both felt that. But –'

'I know she's going over and over the call all the time in her head, and she'll tell me if anything more comes back.'

He nodded, but did not look satisfied. Hazel was the only source and shouldn't be left to remember unaided. Maybe Day thought Hazel was getting an easy time, as a cop's daughter. Harpur sympathised. So far, the police could offer nothing, and

Day knew it. Somewhere inside him would be a burning envy of everyone who had daughters safe at home.

At Ash Tree School, Harpur's panic deepened. Suddenly, here, even the tiny handful of pointers he thought reliable began to look worthless. The headmistress brought Cheryl-Ann's exercise books and he skimmed through them. Here and there on the inside covers she had drawn hearts and arrows, with her own initials and the letters DE intertwined.

'Isn't that a help?' the head asked.

'It means Dark Eyes.'

'Oh, I see. A lot of them about.' She had some notes on her desk. 'I've something I think I can pass on to you.'

She spoke brusquely as if the search for the child was somehow improper and not a matter she should be involved in.

'One of the girls came to see me when we heard about the disappearance today and said she remembered Jennifer speaking of an acquaintance. Well, of a man. We call her Jennifer here, of course, not that other nonsense.'

So, was this the confidante Harpur had been looking for? 'May I see the girl?' He felt hopeful and excited.

'I'm afraid not. Certainly not without the parents' permission. People are very fussy about police interviewing their children. It's reasonable, I think, in view of some rather disturbing cases.'

'Mr and Mrs Day would very much like it if I could interview *their* child.'

'I don't mind passing on to you what the pupil said.'

'Oh, grand.'

'It was a conversation at a school disco, to which pupils from our paired boys' school were invited.' The head looked at the notes. 'Jennifer apparently said she was not really interested in any of the lads present because she had a very secret boyfriend, grown-up, who owned several cars. She said she couldn't invite him to the disco because he went abroad a lot to places like Mozambique looking after his property. That's all.'

'Several cars?'

'That's what she said.'

'What make?'

'I've said, that was all.'

'Property in Mozambique? Who the hell does Mozambique belong to? Christ, I must see this child. It could be fantasy, it could be something real.'

'I could ask the parents, but I should warn you that my recommendation would be that they should decline. I can't have you swearing at children, browbeating them.'

'Well, thanks. Several cars?' he repeated. Jesus. 'Do you realise what this could mean to the search?' He had thought they had it narrowed to an old blue Mercedes with a dud exhaust, or possibly a new exhaust, by now.

'Mr Harpur, if that's all, I have to go and prevent the Press from harassing the children. They've been here with cameras from an early hour.'

'And there's definitely nothing else here that she wrote? Has she a desk, or a locker with a key?'

'All we have, you've seen.' She tidied the exercise books to show it was over. 'Mr Harpur, isn't there something wrong when a man like this can be at large after so many offences?'

'Yes, I think you could say there's something wrong.'

The feeble attempt at sarcasm, or perhaps a special shadow in Harpur's voice, must suddenly have told her of his despair. She stared at Harpur. 'She is still alive, isn't she? Please say so. You could still find her?'

Very young for the job, fat, pretty, full of vigour, all at once she seemed knocked out, as if the possibility that it was too late had not dawned till now. Her hostility evaporated, and the PTA smart-arse superiority. Had this bright woman only recently realised that neither she nor the thoughtful governors of Ash Tree, nor the loaded mothers and fathers of the kids, were going to find Cheryl-Ann, but that Harpur just might? Although she and her mousy lot did not think much of what they would probably call 'the State's law enforcement arm', or worse, they occasionally spotted through a haze of high-mindedness and easy-come scruples that the police they despised were the only police around and so they had better invest a little hope in them.

'Of course we'll find her, ducks,' Harpur said. 'We put out a net, you know, and it's closing all the time.'

'Doesn't it close very slowly?'

'Quicker as we eliminate whole areas and can concentrate.'
Who knew if he was still inside the net?

In turmoil she began to blush. 'Really, I'd like to help you more, but I take my instructions on these matters from the governors. They phoned me first thing this morning.' She pursed her lips. 'Look, as a matter of fact, there is something else that Jennifer wrote which we have here. At first, I thought it was too dark and private for you to see. On consideration, I don't believe there would be any harm. Would you care to look?'

Dark. Private. He would have torn the building apart to find it. 'Only if you have time.'

She went from the room and in a few minutes came back with a valise. From it she took a couple of sheets of paper covered in spiky, childish handwriting. 'This is Jennifer's recent English literature examination.'

Christ, was that all? 'Oh, yes.'

'It does cast a light.'

Let it cast it quickly. 'I was hoping for something else.'

'What sort of thing?'

'Never mind. Please, go ahead.'

'They had to say why they liked the novel *Wuthering Heights*. It's about a strange love affair involving a girl called Catherine – oh, but you've probably read it.'

'No, but I saw the movie.'

'This is what she wrote, at the end.' She began to read in a wrought-up, increasingly breathless voice. '"Their love was everything. Even if they had not been able to speak to each other or meet it would not have mattered because they were like one soul because of their great love. This was the kind of love which people at this time, which is known as the Romantic Age, all believed in." Actually, the Brontës come a bit after, but we don't quibble. "This kind of love can still come for anyone, however, not just Catherine in distant times, and it is wonderful, even if you have never met the other person properly or spoken to him. I know this to be TRUE." Capitals.' The Head's voice began to shake. '"Even death cannot end their love, for it lasts for all time so they continue to seek each other even after death and the grave does not matter, as in this lovely book. This love is when souls are joined for ever. It cannot be broken. I am sure that E. Brontë, who wrote this book, is right about this, I hope so. This is why I like the book, because it has love beyond the grave. Catherine's words are very true in this book, such as: "He is more myself than I am. He's always, always in my mind: not as a pleasure, any more than I am always a pleasure to myself, but as my own being."' The head lowered the papers.

'I recognise that bit. I hope she got a good mark.'

'This child could have gone quite willingly, thinking it was like a story. Jennifer – or I'll call her Cheryl-Ann, just this once – Cheryl-Ann lives in her imagination, or lived in her imagination.'

Eric Day had made the opposite kind of correction, from death to life, but Harpur feared the Head had a better chance of being right.

Driving back to headquarters he wondered whether he had learned anything, except confirmation that on some things the girl was likely to be a romancer and a liar. In school discos she probably did badly for boys, because at that stupid age the lads wouldn't be wowed by beautiful long legs reaching all the way up to a rather melancholy, unpretty face. She might have decided to dig into her make-believe resources and come up with this creature of wealth and mystery. Property in Mozambique, for God's sake. They had probably been doing that slice of the world in geography and she liked the sound.

Then there were the several cars – none of course a big, dark, shattered, old banger with an exhaust like *The Guns of Navarone*. Could he believe any of it, and, if he could, how should it change the direction of the search? What he did believe, and wished he didn't, was the head teacher's suggestion that this child had sprinted voluntarily into hazard because she imagined life was like a bit of classic literature, with herself in the main role. Maybe they ought to stop kids reading that sweaty sort of canonised book and put them on to Harold Robbins where what really happened between a girl and a man was made a little clearer.

He decided to ignore all the disco information and spent the afternoon helping his team frantically work through computer offerings about big cars and sex offences from the time of Lot's daughters. Francis Garland came and sat on the table near him. 'Iles thinks he's got something.'

'Something good?'

They went to Harpur's room.

'We're not supposed to know about it,' Garland said, laughing at the notion that Iles or anyone else could put one over on him: Garland, full of faith in his own powers, most of it justified, could be a screaming pain and an unmatchable help. 'Hubert Scott found something in one of the phone booths we were checking. He put it in his pocket – thought I wasn't looking. Now, Iles is ordering an immediate drag-net in the area. There'll be fifty men, dogs, total seal-off. It starts in an hour.'

'Scott kept you in the dark?'

'Iles must have told him to play things very close. You know what the two Brothers are like.'

'But there was a cooling since Scott let him down at the university.'

'Perhaps Hubert wants to work his way back to favour. Anyway, he was very stealthy. Iles doesn't trust you. When I was seeing his wife she mentioned that. And, obviously, he doesn't think much of me.'

'My God, this is unbelievable – trying to cut us out now, as well as the county.'

'They think they do it better without us. It's the Floss council estate. They're convinced they've got him cornered in the north end. Don't ask me whether the girl's still there, alive.'

'Jesus, they've got to go gingerly.'

'Nothing we can do about it, is there?'

'If they frighten him he could – Iles wants him so much and so fast he might not think about that.'

Garland grinned for a moment, pleased with himself, as ever. 'What Scott found was a Gauloise cigarette, part-smoked, almost snapped in two and with a small bloodstain on it, as if it had fallen from someone's mouth in a struggle. Maybe there was a cut lip. I pickpocketed Scott, to have a look.'

'I should bloody well hope so.'

'And put it back. He doesn't know I've seen it.'

'Does the Lolita Man smoke?'

'Nothing on that. Do we know he's recently been abroad?'

'No, but it's a possibility. You can buy Gauloise here, anyway.'

'Iles is taking charge himself.'

'That's what I was afraid of. Barton know?'

'He will when it's too late to stop it.'

Not long afterwards Harpur met Iles in the Incident Room. The blackboard showed thirty-four. 'You've heard of the little saunter I'm proposing, have you, Col? It's a whim, nothing more. I'm picking an area out with a pin and really going through it. Might be lucky, might not. One does so want to be directly involved, to be doing something in this sort of case. Sitting in an office dealing with public complaints and Civil Defence bumf one repeatedly hears the voice of this child in one's head, calling piteously, and finally one has to answer. Let me have the dummy, would you? I'll put him in a phone box – see if anyone responds.

'I'll be moving with extreme care and I'll have Hubert Scott alongside to remind me of the dos and don'ts of a sweep. He's not such a bad old time-server, after all. We must take care not to panic this bastard. I act believing the girl is still alive, and my only aim to keep it like that. You can tell your bloody contact in the Holy See what's going on if you like, and much sodding good may it do you. I suppose they feed you stuff in exchange, a slimy commerce. You sicken me, Col, but, in the last resort, we are all members of a fine, comradely body, eager to stand by each other whatever may come.'

'It's a bracing creed, sir.'

'What we tried to tell that cow of a reporter. She wouldn't listen. They simply don't know how to cope with ordinary, decent sentiments.'

'Did you get hold of the editor?'

'Surly sod. I think they'll run that rot. Not to worry. I must go.'

'I take it you don't want me up there?'

'A waste of your time, Col. I'm acting irrationally, just for the sake of doing something, anything. Of course, I'll call you right away, should we get a sniff. Reverting, does Lane actually cough anything to you in reciprocity?'

Harpur replied, 'So much contradictory stuff flowing,' if that was a reply.

'So, no he doesn't.'

No, he hadn't, so far.

'I could have warned you, Col. Those sods know how to take, and that's about it. If you can't learn the way to screw them you're stuck for keeps. Maybe that's all you want. Someone like you, you could run community policing, or some estimable crap like that, but you're not front-line. A few more of your sort and we'd never have beaten the miners. For a start, you can't recognise the fucking enemy.'

Now and then in this case, Harpur wondered whether Iles might have it right. On the way home he drove past the edge of the Floss and from a distance watched the operation. It looked neat and subtle. If they really were using dogs the handlers had been told to keep them out of sight and quiet until the call came. Iles needed no coaching from Hubert Scott, and you could see it was not just venom and cricket that had put him where he was.

Megan had not returned from London when he arrived and the girls were putting their school books and swimming gear ready for the morning.

'What's she up to, anyway?' Hazel asked.

'Shopping.'

'Really?'

'What else?'

'You tell us. I hate liberated marriages. It's so dated. This is not the sixties.'

'And unhygienic,' Jill stated.

'Do you ever think about crabs, dad?'

'I'm going to bed for a few hours,' he said. Not long afterwards he heard Megan arrive in a taxi. She climbed into bed and seemed to sleep immediately.

22

It's bad again tonight. I don't sleep any more. Even the pills don't do much good. Another terrible thing happened today, I don't understand it. Well, I could laugh at the police just for a minute and then this terrible thing happened.

Now, when I think about the police I lie here with my mind working and not letting me sleep at all, it is hell. I don't think I should worry, but I do. They've found the telephone box where I had that trouble, this is obvious. Tonight they had police all round it, and I couldn't go back to the box. They must think I live near that box, which was what made me laugh, when my place is miles away down here.

It must have been in that silly trouble with her that I lost my medallion. It's missing and I need it for luck, all gold, my phoenix medallion. I knew she smashed a ciggy out of my mouth but I didn't realise the phoenix had gone. The ciggy didn't seem important, but the phoenix is special. God, I could not go near to look because of all the pigs. Good job I went on the bus because I could see them from upstairs and didn't get off. They were stopping all cars, it could have been very bad.

Well, it's still bad because the phoenix is important, showing it doesn't matter how bad things seem you can win. Now, I don't feel like I'm winning. All I have is pain and my mind working and not able to rest. I looked down from the bus just when I was going to get off and saw all the men and cars and then in the phone box, just standing there, I saw myself again, like that day in the car.

I was wearing my grey leather bomber jacket, not holding the phone, or anything like that, just standing, like leaning against the glass. It's like the past coming alive suddenly in front of you, you are going over something in your life like a dream. But I was on the bus and I could feel the torn seat and the metal on the edge of the seat, it was real. I was just getting up to get off, holding the handrail, when I saw all the people and then myself. I sat down again. I was scared people on the bus would notice.

It's like going mad, when you know you're in one place, and can feel the torn seat and the metal, and you see yourself somewhere else. It's like having a fever. Oh, Jesus, my mind. It is always working and working, but am I sick there? They said on the TV news I was sick in the head and I didn't believe it, they can go fuck theirselves, but is it true? Sometimes I want to end everything. If you keep on seeing yourself somewhere else you don't know what's real, and this can be a sign of being mad, can't it?

23

Jill awoke Harpur and Megan with a cup of tea at nearly eight o'clock next morning. Dismayed that he had slept so late, Harpur left the bed at once. When he looked at the clock it was as if he saw Iles's blackboard. Now it would be reading only twenty-three.

As he dressed, the phone rang and Megan stirred slowly and picked it up. She listened for a while and said: 'My husband's not here. Been out since before dawn.' She dropped the receiver back. 'BBC,' she told him. 'They wanted to talk to you about some London newspaper story that says your lot and Ethan's are dangerously hampering each other in the search for Cheryl-Ann. Sounds bloody well-informed.'

'What sort of day did you have in the Smoke?'

'Good fun. Tiring.' She lay back. 'Sorry.'

'What?'

'Oh, I don't know – it seems wrong to skip off like that when you're deep into this horror. I'll go and see Sybil today. Is there any –?'

'I don't think so. I'd have heard.'

'How are they?'

'Eric seemed more or less OK. Sybil kept out of the way.'

'I shan't know what to say to them, Col.'

'Say there's still a chance.'

'A chance of what?'

'Finding her alive. Kids can recover from anything.'

'Is it true – that she could be alive?'

'Of course it bloody is.'

'Don't shout. It makes you sound as if you don't really believe it.'

The girls wanted a lift to school. Hazel, in the back, said just as they were starting: 'What's this?' and held up a box she had found in the seat.

'You left your snorkel at the Days' place. Cheryl-Ann's father gave it to me.'

'No, I didn't. I packed mine last night for swimming today. I've got it here in my duffle bag.'

'The box Mr Day gave me has your initials on it.' They began to move.

'Oh. I must have picked up Cheryl-Ann's by mistake. They were all in that shed thing. We put them on the shelf alongside hers.' In the mirror he saw her pull an identical Dolfino box out of her bag. 'Sorry. You're right, dad. This isn't mine. Oh, there's a green book under the mask.'

'Leave hers in the car, then, and take your own to swimming,' he said. He drove fast, still appalled to have lost so much of the morning.

In a while Hazel said suddenly: '"He is more myself than I am. He's always, always in my mind: not as a pleasure, any more than I am always a pleasure to myself, but as my own being."'

Bewildered and chilled to hear her speak those words used in Cheryl-Ann's examination paper he glanced in the mirror again and saw she was reading from the green-covered book.

'I know that stuff,' Hazel said. 'She must have copied it out of a cranky story called *Wuthering Heights*. Schoolmistresses think it's orgasmic and everybody has to do it and learn chunks.'

'What are you reading from?' Harpur asked. 'It's not *Wuthering Heights*?'

'I think it's Cheryl-Ann's diary, dad, and it ought to be private,' Jill replied. 'She must have hidden it in the snorkel box to keep it secret, and it's not right to read it.'

'Well, yes, it ought to be private normally,' Hazel told her, 'but this is different, you great berk. A diary could tell us vital things about people she knew, and so on, couldn't it, dad?'

'I don't think you should read it,' Jill said.

'Nor do I,' Harpur told her. 'Put it back in the box, please, Hazel.'

'So you can read it when we're gone? There's registration numbers and things about car makes, all to do with some guy who's been watching her, he sounds creepy. And things about a certain police officer. She doesn't like you.'

'You mustn't mention this, Hazel.'

'Are you scared the famous Mr Iles will hear and pinch all the glory? Oh, dad, the diary is terribly sad. She thought he was wonderful. She calls him "wonderful he" all the time. And look what has happened to her.'

'We don't know.'

'Lots of girls actually get married to people they think is wonderful he and find it's different,' Jill stated.

'Thank you, vicar,' Hazel snarled.

In his office he read the diary's last entries first. 'I could not seek him today. Fate was against it,' and then, later, 'Tomorrow I really shall be free to seek him and nothing can go wrong.'

He had never wept during any case and he didn't weep now before this strange, laboured handwriting, as gawky as the girl herself. They were words on a page, and that was all. Just the same, some of those words hit him hard. He heard the voice of the child, thrilled, determined, doomed. 'Nothing can go wrong.' She had slept that night, or, more likely, failed to sleep, full of the certainty that she was due to move from her dreaming and romancing to reality at last. And she was right, tragically and horribly right. She thought love could be spirits communing from beyond the grave, and here was the Lolita Man waiting to tear her open and leave her broken.

He heard the voice of the child, but it was not really the language of a child. Who said 'seek' these days, or 'thereupon'? Who talked about a room being 'ever rich' with the smell of some scent? This girl lifted words from stuff she had read because she thought her love had to be written about in a special, fancy way. This kid believed Fate was her enemy because Fate gave a bad time to so many of the great lovers in stories. Maybe you could call it Fate that got the Lolita Man going, but there were better, clinical words.

The diary said the girl thought he had come to seek her in her scented room, and she was probably right. To her that was a lovely idea, a kind of closeness. But it must have meant he was almost out of control then, so cock-happy he would take any risk to get at her. Already she had recorded that he looked bad, and the day after she went out at first light and put it on a plate for him because heroines always sought their heroes, no matter how much Fate tried to put the stopper on.

Because his training said the last information counted most, he continued reading the later entries first. He reached the description of her visit to his house, when she met Hazel and Jill. 'Their father is police . . . and he began asking a lot of questions which I didn't like . . . the questions were like he knew something about us, yet this is not possible.' Too bloody true. He knew next to nothing then and not much more now.

He read on and slowly anger with the diary began to replace his feelings of sadness and pity. Why did she never write anything concrete? There was all this mad, over-heated language but no names. The childish guff grew stifling. Hazel had said something about car registrations, hadn't she? Where the hell were they?

Barton came in carrying a newspaper and put it on Harpur's desk. 'Who gives a twopenny fuck for this?' he said. He was wearing an old navy-blue blazer and a club rugby tie.

Harpur read the front-page headline. LOLITA DEATHS: SCANDAL OF POLICE OBSTRUCTION. There were pictures of the Chief and Ethan, both in uniform, Ethan captioned 'prominent Catholic' and Barton 'long-time Mason'. The opening paragraph, under the girl reporter's name, began: 'The search for 14-year-old Cheryl-Ann Day, believed a prisoner of the vicious sex-killer known as the Lolita Man, is being hampered by bitter rivalry between top officers of the two police forces involved, one led by Catholics, the other by Freemasons. Time could be running out for the pretty schoolgirl, yet resources which could have been devoted to the search have been diverted to this running inter-Force battle.' Under a photograph of Iles, also in uniform, was a one-word caption, 'Intrigue'.

'All this is not going to matter, Col.' The Chief's voice was too high. 'This sweep by Iles will turn out good. I feel it. They've got a real pointer, you know. I can tell you it's a bloodstained cigarette, indicating a struggle in a telephone booth. This is first-rate detective work. On an estate like that it will be slow going, but it will come. They've been working all night.'

Harpur put the girl's diary into his drawer.

'Desmond wants to handle this thing at the Floss by himself, Colin. All right, it's not usual for an ACC, but there are exceptional matters at stake. I certainly don't want you to feel left out, and neither does Desmond. He said that to me particularly. Look, I know I spoke to you differently about Desmond not long ago – asking you to exclude him if you could – but this press shit changes things. Read that right through and you'll see it's grossly slanted against us. Every damn word. We're the ones who are supposed to be sitting on stuff, endangering this child and more or less promoting the deaths of the others. It's cruel and mendacious. Ethan and Lane come out of it like long-suffering fucking saints. Who owns this rag, a Mick? Obviously the whole thing had been fed them by that skinny lecher, Ethan. It's to put a smoke-screen over the balls he made on their arrest. There's some totally foul allegation about Desmond having instigated a shit-dig into Lane's background – something to do with racial prejudice when he was a student. As if Desmond would hold that against anybody. It actually names poor old Hubert Scott as being sent to Lane's university to collect damaging material. You can see why Desmond thought he must score, and thank God he's going to. If anyone can bring this off, Desmond can.

'That swine of a reporter pulls every trick against him, suggesting his wife spreads it about. What's the usual libel-dodging code – "fun-loving and very companionable"? We'll have the laugh tomorrow when this lot have to print we've caught the bloody Lolita Man. Do you think the bastards will put that on the front page?' He looked away from the paper.

'How about you, Col? I popped in to see whether you'd turned up anything.'

'We're still badgering the computer, sir.'

'Someone's going to stumble over a corpse very soon. I don't believe that bloody blackboard any longer, do you?'

'There's no pattern, sir. The blackboard was a bit of optimism from the start. But it could still be right.'

'Yes.' He nodded with a sudden show of spirit. 'Yes, of course it could be.' Taking the newspaper he drew it across his buttocks and dropped it in the waste-paper bin.

As soon as he had gone, Harpur began swiftly reading the diary right through from the beginning, occasionally making a note. At the end he rang for Francis Garland, handed the book to him and watched while he absorbed it.

'The girl's, sir? Christ, how did you get it?'

'Just plod.'

'Brilliant. Personalised number plates! He advertises! We've got the bugger, haven't we? I take it you've asked the computer who he is. A Lagonda, a Ferrari, an Aston – so he's loaded, or working in a vintage car museum. Some rich sod indulging his kinks. He's on toast. We move now?'

'This kid has dreams, Francis.'

Garland looked confused and took a while to answer. 'Well, maybe. But she's gone. That's not a dream. Are you saying there's no bloke?'

'Bits of it are real.'

'Which bits?'

'I'm not sure.'

'Well, then –'

'Not the cars. Not the number plates.'

'How the hell can you tell?'

Garland would not enjoy being accused of naïvety.

'A feeling,' Harpur said.

Garland rang the computer unit and asked them to get the owners of DE1, DE2 and DE3. He hung on. 'Thanks,' he said, and replaced the receiver. 'No such registrations. I suppose you'd already checked. God, this is like working on ciphers. So, it's totally useless, the diary?'

Harpur pushed towards him the couple of notes he had made.

'Some things are repeated time and again. I'd bet they're right. All the cars are blue.'

'That ties with that we've had all along. The chambermaid at the King Richard picked out a picture of an old Humber or Mercedes and said blue.'

'Yes, I've got other information to suggest a blue Mercedes – ancient, disintegrating. Cheryl-Ann had to confer a bit of opulence on him, and so the Lagonda, and what not.'

'She keeps on about smoking, so Iles could be right about the Gauloise.'

'Yes.'

'Sod him.'

'The medallion is probably OK and the suntan. And I'd bet he's clean-shaven. The Monix shirt sounds like something she's copied from a colour magazine.'

Garland was flicking the pages. 'What's the rosy chorus about "always, always in my mind" and him being part of her?'

'I think I remember that from one of the Brontës, don't I? Maybe *Wuthering Heights*.'

'I didn't know you were a reader, sir.'

'If we have a literary heritage, use it, that's what I always say.'

'Is that what you always say, sir?'

Harpur's phone rang. 'This could be Iles to report he's got him and would we like to come up now and applaud.'

It was Mark Lane. 'Could we meet?'

'When?'

'Right away.'

'Where?'

'You know the Old Lock pub?'

'Fine.'

When Harpur rang off Garland asked: 'Something private, sir?'

'You know how it is. Look, Francis, I'd like you to go up to the Floss. I'm scared stiff for the girl now, if Iles is getting close. We could have a hostage situation. Iles won't let me anywhere near it.'

'He's not too fond of me.'

'We've got to try it. I must have someone subtle up there.' That ought to sell him the idea.

'What will you do?' Garland asked.

Harpur locked up the diary. 'I'm going to assume the suntan and the Gauloise do mean something. It's possible he works abroad, not Mozambique, maybe, but it could be Europe or on a rig. We've wondered before if that would explain the long spells of quiet and the leave periods when he watched his targets. I'll see if the Foreign Office and the Department of Employment will come up with some sort of list. We could pull out young men from this area.'

Garland went and Harpur drove at once into next door's territory to meet Lane. It was a quaint, smart, small, riverside hotel and Harpur soon saw why Lane had chosen it. A mobile crane was working from the bank and, as Harpur parked, he heard it start to strain and lift. The roof of a car broke surface. It looked like a big, old, blue Mercedes. Christ, had they searched it? Had they recovered anyone?

Lane was seated alone in a corner of the bar, with a Scotch ready for Harpur. 'Someone heard a vehicle go in during the night and may have seen a man hoofing it away afterwards. We've had a diver down and the cabin is empty. But he couldn't open the boot.'

Jesus. 'Has it got plates?'

'Yes. The car was stolen more than four months ago in Wales.' He drank and Harpur bought a couple more. Lane went on: 'Ethan's in London today on a terrorism committee. It's a bit of luck. The phone boxes produced bugger all for us, but I felt I owe you.'

'Thanks.'

'We're going to have to open the boot in a minute. We'd better face it. The girl could be in there.'

They went outside. The Mercedes hung clear now and as they watched was gently lowered to the bank. A couple of men moved forward with crowbars.

'Just a minute,' Lane ordered. 'We'll need a screen, for God's sake.'

People had come out of the hotel to watch. A couple of police vans were quickly placed near the car and tarpaulins hung carefully between them.

'OK now,' Lane said.

Harpur tried to visualise what had happened in the night, and then tried not to. As Iles's massive, inspired search grew closer and closer to him, the Lolita Man might have been driven frantic by fear. He would realise that the girl and probably his car would be the biggest give-aways. So, had he piled Cheryl-Ann into the boot, maybe alive, maybe not, and come here secretly to lose both? Even if Iles was in the wrong spot, that could still be the scenario. It looked as if the Lolita Man had begun to panic. As the boot lid went up, Harpur turned his back.

In a while Lane said: 'Only the spare.'

'Sorry for playing Mr Sensitive.' Harpur took his jacket off and examined the car's underside. In the exhaust he found a hole as big as a medal, and the pipe had been lashed to the body-work with what looked like new wire. 'Could be,' he told Lane.

'We'll get pictures of it on television. I know that might scare him even more, but it's so late we'll have to risk it.'

'Agreed.' Harpur pulled out the car's ashtray. The stubs were all Gauloise. Cheryl-Ann had always known smoking might catch up with him. 'What did you think of our Press this morning?'

Lane yawned. 'I try not to read the papers. Don't they dramatise everything, though?' He looked at his watch. 'We must meet again soon. I could come to your side next time. Equal partners, and all that.'

By the time Harpur returned to the Incident Room in mid-afternoon, Iles's board had just been changed to fourteen. Garland was back from the Floss. 'Iles threw me off the operation. "No help needed from licentious fucking quislings." He's into one of his spells. It looks as if things have gone cold up there all of a sudden. Perhaps he knows they're not going to get him, and didn't want me around smirking.'

'God, the Floss was our best bet.'

'That's why he's so cut-up: one minute roses, the next sack-cloth, like life itself. He's even had a row with poor old Hubert Scott and told him to get lost, too, although he's Grand

Master, or whatever. Something about not doing a proper job at Warwick University and failing to check buses last night, only cars. Apparently Iles believes the Lolita Man does his jobs by public transport.'

'It's not so dim. This lad was getting scared about his car, that's clear now.'

'Anyway, Scott's livid. His name is in the paper over the smear trip to Warwick and he's not at all keen on that. Look, sir, it seems he found something else when he picked up the Gauloise, but didn't show it to Iles, was going to work on it himself. You know the nasty, secretive ways these old CID people have. Now he's saying "Sod Iles" and "Sod the case." He gave it to me.' Garland opened his hand to disclose a medallion, the kind worn around the neck with an open shirt by all sorts of Narcissuses.

'Gold?'

'Solid. Think of it with one of those Monix creations as worn by the pop stars.'

'The magical bird, isn't it?'

'A charm against lung cancer. The phoenix will arise from the ash.'

'The jeweller might be traceable. Perhaps he'll remember the sale, even have a record.'

'I've been ringing around, sir. So far I've hit nobody who stocks them.'

'He might have bought it abroad. Keep plodding, though, Francis.'

Harpur telephoned the Foreign Office and the Department of Employment to ask for a list of people working abroad from the area. They both wanted to know which country, and when he said he didn't know, but somewhere that would give a heavy sun-tan, the conversation died. He could see their point.

Despair began to tear at him again. There had seemed to be a sudden spurt of movement, but now it was over. Had he reached another dead-end, like Iles? Useless self-recriminations gnawed: why hadn't he started looking for the jeweller as soon as he read about the medallion in the diary?

In a short while the pictures of the ditched Mercedes would come up on television and calls would flood in from all over, half from nutters, some from pranksters, even in a case like this, some from villains planning an outing tonight and wanting to send the police elsewhere, a few from people who meant well but had made a little error about the car make or the registration or where they actually saw it. All the calls would have to be logged and checked by patrols: no way of computerising this. It would be tomorrow before the rubbish was hacked away and a short-list of real possibles made. And, by then, all the seventy-two hours allowed to find the girl would be gone, if the seventy-two hours had really been on offer in the first place.

In case he had missed something, he re-read the diary from front to back. Was it fact or a bit of Prince Charming cliché that the Lolita Man had big shoulders and might train on weights? Would it be worth a tour of the gyms, or were his work-outs done in the recreation centre of some oil installation in Libya or the Emirates? Was she right about the hair-do? Had it been done locally? Would one of the so-called stylists remember that momentous session when this customer's dark glory was lifted from off his forehead, making him a new man, but still one who liked destroying young girls?

He put the diary back in its Dolfino box under the mask. Somehow the silliness of so much of it, the hot, concocted breathlessness, made him ashamed to be reading these pages. Jill had been right: the entries were private. Hazel had been right too, of course: the diary could have provided facts capable of saving Cheryl-Ann's life. That was still possible. The medallion might turn out important, and the smoking, even the haircut. Yes, possible, just about.

All the same, he did not want it known he had intruded on the girl's secrets, the make-believe ones or the real, if any were real. He would not like her mother and father to find out about it, and especially not that sad, stiff figure, Eric Day. Harpur had felt bad enough turning over the girl's bedroom. This was worse.

He took the box out to his car and drove up to near the Days' house. Then he spent all the early part of the evening banging doors in the neighbourhood, asking if people had seen the blue Mercedes about at any time. This was better than waiting for calls to be sorted out after the TV item. Doorstep detective work always comforted him at bad moments. The slowness, the laboriousness, the lack of technology could make him think this was the genuine hard slog and that he was not sparing himself. It deserved success, earned it. Earning was not the same as getting, though. He kept at this work until after 11 p.m., but without result. It had grown dark and people were beginning to go to bed. He returned to the car, took the Dolfino box and went on foot up to the Days' house and into their garden. Lights burned still in the big lounge behind drawn curtains. Did the Days know about the seventy-two hour span the police put on their daughter's life? Were they aware the figure was down to six now? Would either of them sleep tonight?

Carefully opening the door to the changing shed he put the box on a shelf with the other gear, closed up again and left. Maybe there would be another report of a thuggish and threatening-looking prowler around the Days' house. That description must have gone deep. It had been in his head while he fingered the diary and was one reason he felt so ashamed of breaking open her little secrets.

Still on foot he went to Canberra Avenue and Ruth's place. 'I thought you might turn up tonight,' she said.

'Why?'

'Things are bad, aren't they? You look pretty sick. I hoped you'd need me.'

'Yes, I do. Does it make you seem like a service, someone to minister to my self-pity?'

'Once in a while is OK. After all, you've done the same for me. You're not generally into misery.'

He had hung the radio on a chair as usual but tonight the interruption came on her phone downstairs. The ringing did not go away.

'It might wake the kids,' she said, climbing out of bed. 'Have you given someone this number?'

'You must be joking.'

She went down to answer and in a minute returned. 'Francis Garland. I asked him what made him think you'd be here and he said, "Acting on information received."'

Harpur dressed in case one of the children had been awoken and started wandering. Christ, this house wasn't kitted for an adulterer who worked late. She would have to get a bedside extension.

'Salaams,' Garland began. 'Don't fret. I tried here before your house.'

'Bright.'

'My personal assessment forms always say so. There's something good on the phoenix medallion. I've been calling on jewellers at home. One of them sold something like our exhibit to a woman last October. He does insurance for customers, so there's a name and address.'

'What sort of woman?'

'Early twenties, he thinks. It looks as if our boy might have had something normal going, as well as the taste for kids. That's classic, isn't it? Standard sex is available but not enough.'

'We all know that feeling. Has this woman claimed on the insurance?'

'What?'

'If she's lost it, or had it nicked.'

'She may have given it as a present.'

'That's what I'm trying to work out. So she hasn't claimed?'

'He didn't say so.'

'You didn't ask?'

'All right, I should have. One up to you. Look, sir, I'm on my way to the address now.'

'I'd better come.'

'There's a snag.'

'Not on our ground?'

'Bright.'

'The Warden of All Souls said so.'

'But we can't hand this over, sir. I –'

'Oh, we've got to do it ourselves.'

'Great. Might we need help?'

'You mean dogs and fifty people?'

'OK, we do it alone.'

'You could invite Hubert Scott. He gave us the lead. We owe him. Got his number?'

'I never thought of you as a bridge-builder, sir. Not a saboteur, either. An isolationist.'

'I've had lessons in hands-across-the-sea from Lane. Give me the address. We'll rendezvous at 2 a.m. outside.'

Then, still building bridges, he rang Lane and offered him a welcome to this clandestine meeting on his own patch.

It was a flat over a television rental shop in a grubby, crowded district, not at all bad for a hideout. Few people around here would make a habit of reporting what they saw to the police and screams from a flat would be par for the course. When Harpur arrived Garland and Scott were already in position.

Scott said: 'No sign of life, sir. One staircase at the rear. A nothing door and locks. And thanks for including me in.'

'Christ, the fuzz,' Garland muttered as Lane drew up.

'You told him?' Scott asked Harpur incredulously. 'If I'd known you'd do that I'd never –'

'The register gives a Deborah Mary Fletcher and Robert George Aix at this address,' Lane said.

'Yes, I got Fletcher from the jeweller,' Garland told them.

Was Robert George Aix also Mr Dark Eyes and the Lolita Man, wonderful, wonderful he, then? Was he sleeping the sleep of the deviously satisfied? What part did the woman play? Harpur grew excited and apprehensive. 'I don't like the idea of just knocking and waiting.' He felt the same fear as in the Iles operation: if they did not act quickly enough this man might grab a hostage.

'Knock and don't wait then,' Lane replied at once. 'We'll lean on their door for a bit of a rest. All these buggers, snoring on their Dunlopillos – they can't begrudge us a short lean, surely to God.'

Harpur sensed Scott begin to warm to him then. What did it matter whether he did or not? Scott was here to make up numbers, a grace and favour guest, an Iles discard. The four of them went quickly up the stairs and Lane immediately put his shoulder to the door, rocked back and shoved. The lock burst.

They were in a small corridor, empty except for coats on wall pegs. Splintered lino and soiled mats made the floor covering. Cheryl-Ann was used to better.

'Police,' Lane bellowed. 'Debbie? Robert? Cheryl-Ann?

Keep still everyone. We're coming in. Don't be disturbed. Only a routine visit about crime prevention.'

From one of the rooms a man yelled something, maybe a curse, maybe a question and Harpur dashed past Lane towards the sound and opened a door. Garland and Scott hurried to cover the rest of the place.

A man wearing underpants was out of bed and stood facing Harpur, fists ready. Behind, a woman had begun to sit up in the double bed and turned her head away from the beam of Harpur's flashlight. The man suddenly reached behind him into the darkness, picked up a glass vase and smashed it on the dressing table, scattering water and old flowers. The staleness of the room grew staler. Then he turned to face Harpur again, the weapon held out in front of him, its jagged edges towards Harpur's neck.

'We're looking for a child,' Harpur said, but that did not stop him.

'Who are you? What do you want?'

'Police.'

'Who says?'

'I've got a card.'

'Stuff it.' He lunged with the vase and Harpur backed quickly.

Shoving Harpur violently to one side, Lane rushed forward holding a woman's coat, like someone trying to smother a fire. Before the man could react to him, Lane threw the coat on the vase stub and at the same time, getting very close, hit him a heavy crack with his elbow on the side of the jaw so that Aix slewed and collapsed suddenly on to one knee. Lane seemed about to punch him in the face, finish him, but instead bent down and yanked him to his feet by the skin of his shoulders and forced him to stand, pushing him against the wall. The vase stayed on the floor under the coat.

Changing his grip to the throat, Lane said: 'Why bring disaster on yourself, Robert? We're not even interested in you, you lump of flotsam. Who are you, boy?'

He was nothing like any known description of the Lolita Man: about twenty, very fair, long-haired, thin, bony, big-nosed, big-chinned.

'You're Robert George Aix?' Lane asked.

'Is there anyone else here?' Harpur said.

'What?'

'A girl?'

'What girl?'

'Your shoulders are not right.'

'What? I done nothing.'

'Threatening an officer with broken glass?' Lane replied. 'Grave. And don't I smell grass above the general aroma of decay? Fifth-quality, but grass all the same.'

'You got no right in here. It was self-defence, that's all. How did I know who you are?'

'The door was open,' Lane said. 'We came up to make sure you were all right. It suddenly struck us as we were passing that Debbie and Robert might have left their front door open and we thought we'd better see you were all right. And here you are, all right. Ever think of changing your underwear?'

Garland and Scott came back from their tour of the flat and Garland shook his head.

'Show Deborah the gold, Francis,' Harpur said.

She had pulled on a kind of dressing gown and was sitting on the side of the bed, still trying to bring herself round and get her eyes to focus. Perhaps Lane was right and there had been smokes last night. Well, come out of the sweet dreams cloud, Debbie. We've had enough of those, and time is very short. They switched on a light and Garland sat near her and put the medallion on the coverlet.

'See that before, sweetie?' he asked. 'Think hard. Take your time, but not too much of it. A life might depend on this.'

She stared at it and looked nervous.

'You know it?'

'What life?'

Lane released Aix, who put some clothes and shoes on and was about to leave the room when Scott prevented him.

'Where are you going, Robert?' Lane asked.

'I'm calling a solicitor.'

'It's nearly 3 a.m. He'll be out on the job, they're notorious for that. We don't need him, son. It would only cost you. This is going to be very quick.'

'The middle of the night – we got rights. My heart's weak.'

'Well, take it easy or you'll turn this into another of those cardiac arrests.'

'I'll make a bloody complaint.'

'I handle complaints. Most people say I'm understanding. A real softy.'

Debbie said: 'It's the phoenix, isn't it?'

'Yours?' Garland asked.

'Well, it could be.' She, too, was fair and about the man's age, but burly, her features a little crowded together and maybe off-centre. She would be a special taste.

'Don't answer nothing, Deb,' Aix told her. 'You don't have to. They'll give you all sorts of tales only to tie you up. I seen it before.'

'I bet you have,' Scott said.

'I paid for that medallion,' Debbie whispered.

'We know you did, love,' Harpur said. 'No question of that. What we want to find out is where it went after you bought it. You could save a child.'

'What child?'

'A missing girl.'

'What's the phoenix to do with that?'

'Take our word for it, will you?' Garland replied. 'We don't want to hang about.'

'It's a trick, Deb,' Aix said. 'Believe nothing.'

'Why don't you start tidying up this rag-and-bone shop while we're talking to Debbie?' Lane asked.

'What child?' she repeated.

'Did you give the phoenix to someone?' Garland asked. 'Tell us who and we can be away. That's all it is. Somehow the phoenix seems to have got to a man.'

She lowered her head and mumbled something. Harpur bent to hear. 'It's a bit, well, awkward,' she said.

Aix bent to listen, also. Harpur could see him begin to understand. Aix's face grew threatening. 'Listen, is there another guy in this?' he asked.

She said: 'It was only –'

'You give another guy real gold?'

'What happened, love?' Garland asked.

126

'Come on, we'll go and make a cup of tea,' Scott told Aix, and took his arm.

'No, I stay.' Aix broke from him. 'I got a right to hear this.'

'God, you and rights,' Scott said.

'Who's this guy you give real gold to, Deb? That thing must have really cost. What was he doing for you so you had to give him real gold?'

She looked up at Aix sadly. 'I bought it for you, didn't I, Rob?'

'You what?'

'Our anniversary, first year. We been together twenty months now, off and on,' she told Harpur.

'Nice.'

'I never seen no medallion.'

'No, something went wrong, didn't it?'

'You had a tiff?' Lane asked. 'You broke up for a while?'

She nodded. 'About a week. You walked out, Rob. Remember? I can't even recall what it was about. Money, I suppose. It's always about that.'

Aix said: 'Yes, you spent all –'

'Some of it was to buy the phoenix.'

'And when he went you met someone else?' Harpur asked.

'Only temp'ry. I didn't even know if Rob was ever coming back, did I?'

'Of course not.'

Garland looked at his watch, but there was good stuff here, and they would have to wait.

'So I'm away a couple of days and you've got some other guy in? Charming.'

She began to plead. 'It wasn't like you think. He never touched me. I wouldn't have that, you've got to believe it. Please, Rob. It was just a bit of a smoke, some records. He didn't even try to touch me like that. I think he was funny, you know?'

'Yes, he's funny,' Lane said. 'That's why we've got to find him quickly.' It was getting light.

'He had a name?' Scott asked gently.

'Well, Dave, that was all.'

'Did he look like this?' Harpur asked, bringing out a mug shot of the dummy.

'A bit. Not such good skin.'

'Only a first name?' Garland said.

'He only come here once. I met him in a pub, like. We were both on our own. We got talking and he said call him Dave. He said he worked abroad a lot.'

'Did he talk about girls?' Garland asked. 'Young girls?'

'No. Course not.'

'Did he have a car?' Harpur asked.

'Yes, a big old thing.'

'Merc?' Lane asked.

'Could be.'

'Blue?' Harpur said.

'I think so.'

'You slag, Deb. You picks up some berk in a boozer and brings him back here right away.'

Once again Lane seemed about to hit him, and once again drew back. 'Try not to be mean-minded, Robert, would you? What's a girl supposed to do, sit around waiting for you to decide in your gracious way to come back?'

'You had a smoke and danced to some records, and then he went?' Garland asked.

She nodded.

'And he helped himself from your handbag on the way out, did he?' Lane said.

'Money and the medallion.'

'Did he ever say where he lived?' Harpur asked.

She hesitated. 'This is going to land him in it, yes?'

'For Christ's sake, he screws kids and kills them,' Garland told her.

She still hesitated but then seemed to decide to speak. 'He said down the Pavilions. I don't know if he was there permanent. They comes and goes down there, some do. Others, no, they got goats and lettuce and all that. Is he messing about with kids, then?'

'This happened eight months ago?' Harpur asked.

'Yes. Our anniversary is October.'

It would be just about the time he started.

'You brings an odd-ball back here as soon as I'm out of the door. I don't like that, Deborah.'

'Why didn't you claim on the insurance?' Garland asked.

'I didn't want no investigators coming up here, did I? We was back together.' She smiled. 'I didn't want Rob upset, like he's upset now. But if it's really for a kid –'

'Good girl,' Lane told her. 'Robert's not going to mess you about when we're gone, are you, Robert? I'll be looking in again, probably. I've got a deep, nice feeling you're going to be reasonable.'

'Of course he is,' Harpur said. 'And we'll be able to bring the phoenix back when it's all over. Rob will be able to have it for your second anniversary, maybe. Don't worry, it's holding its value.'

'And best wishes from all of us for many more anniversaries,' Lane said. 'Just stick a chair or something against the door when we've gone. You probably needed a new lock there, anyway.' He put £10 on the bed. 'That should do it.'

Aix picked up the note.

They left. The Pavilions were back on Harpur's ground, a strung-out collection of decaying summer huts in a wood along the coast, built just after the war by a landowner for letting to holiday-makers. The scheme had never taken off and gradually the summer houses were abandoned. Now, hippies and druggies and flat-earthers and back-to-the-land families lived there free, only emerging to collect their giros and occasionally do a bit of small-time thieving. It was one of the first places searched in any sweep, but the alarm system there was better than the Bank of England's. Although the Pavilions were dotted over a square mile of woodland, everyone knew as soon as police approached any of them. It beat even the bush telegraph on the Ernest Bevin council estate, where so many of Harpur's crooked regulars lived. To do the Pavilions properly you would need a couple of hundred men.

'Shall we try there again?' Garland asked.

'What else?' Harpur said.

'Right,' Lane agreed. 'May I have permission to enter your ground, kind sir?'

They drove fast back across the boundary. By seven-thirty

they had roused four of the huts, searched them and shown the pictures to people who refused to speak or said they had never seen anyone like him. It would be no good telling them about the girl or the urgency: like Aix these folk did not talk to police and did not believe police. They had about another thirty-five chalets to do, and already Harpur could hear cars and vans and motor bikes out of sight starting up as inhabitants who didn't care to meet the law left for the day or longer. By 9 a.m. they had done six more. It was hopeless.

Harpur's handset spoke and he listened. Then he called the others. 'Iles has found the girl. She's alive. The doctor is with her now.'

'And they've got the Lolita Man?' Garland asked.

'They didn't say.'

'Did you ask?'

'When was this?' Lane said.

'About two hours ago.'

'That clever bastard, Iles,' Garland said.

24

An impromptu press conference developed in the large lounge of the pub opposite St Mary's Hospital, where Cheryl-Ann had been taken. It was Barton himself who proposed it, as a way of clearing the mass of reporters and photographers and broadcasting people from the hospital reception hall and taking the pressure off staff there. Perhaps it was the joyous press conference after the Yorkshire Ripper's capture which influenced the Chief. Could he have forgotten the criticism for being over-hasty which followed that display?

In fact, happy and expansive now the girl was safe, he had probably not thought out very clearly at all what he was doing. The Press would certainly come to the conference. That did not mean they would go away afterwards, though. And there were complications. Barton had not foreseen the simmering anger and resentment of most of the journalists present. The Chief had never really understood the media. He still thought their job was to report speeches, even his. The occasional piece of investigative unpleasantness, like the front page about the inter-Force vendetta, he tried to pretend was an aberration.

Like a benevolent squire, he stood before a boar-hunting tapestry in the bar and issued the half-truths or less that he thought would satisfy all present. 'Ladies and gentlemen, I'm most happy to say that the girl, Jennifer Day, or Cheryl-Ann as she likes to be called – and why not if she wishes it? – is safe and reasonably well, in the circumstances. Her parents, Mr and Mrs Eric Day, personal friends of mine, who are here now, have seen her and spoken to her and found her quite cheerful – again, given the circumstances. The girl was found at around seven-forty this morning as the result of exceptionally vigilant police work, the kind of devoted effort which has characterised the entire difficult case, I'm glad to say. We shall hope to receive good information from Jennifer as soon as the doctors allow us to talk to her and we trust this will lead to a very speedy arrest. We intend to keep you informed, naturally, of every development as soon as it occurs, through our public relations department. Please don't hesitate to contact them. Thank you.'

Harpur saw that this attempt to sound friendly and generous was not going to work.

A woman in denim with cameras slung about her said, 'Is it true, Mr Barton, that one photographer has already been allowed to take pictures of the girl?'

The Chief smiled and nodded. 'I understand Mr and Mrs Day have come to some sort of arrangement with one London newspaper. You should address your questions to them.'

'Have you sold your daughter's story, Mr Day, Mrs Day?' the woman asked.

Eric Day answered in what he tried to make an offhand tone, as if no great issue were involved: 'We thought it best, as a way of avoiding constant pressure on our child from all the media, to hand over totally to one paper, yes.'

'So the rest of us are not going to get a sniff, are we?'

Iles said: 'Oh, as the Chief has promised, we'll keep you informed of all the main developments, of course.'

'But seeing the child, getting pictures?'

'We haven't seen Jennifer ourselves yet,' Barton replied, 'except for Mr Iles and other officers early today.'

'Are you happy to sell the account of your daughter's horrifying experiences, Mr Day, for, what is it, £30,000?' some beaten London reporter asked.

'This way we'll have control over what is written,' Day replied. 'How this matter is reported could affect the rest of our daughter's life.'

'What makes you think you'll have any control?'

'It is part of the contract.'

'So it might be.'

'I shall insist,' Day declared loudly. 'Whereas, in a free-for-all —'

'It's the "free" bit that gets you, is it?' the reporter asked. 'Would you tell us, is the fee the £30,000 we've heard?'

'The money is really irrelevant,' Day replied.

'Oh, sure.'

Iles said: 'As I understand it, the whole amount will go to Cheryl-Ann.'

'Naturally,' Day added.

'Does she know about the deal?'

'Of course,' Iles replied. 'Again, as I understand it, she wanted the arrangement. When Mr Day told her the proposition and the amount she said, "That's a lot of bread in times of unemployment."'

If she had that kind of way with a phrase why on earth had she bothered to lift the gush from Brontë? But maybe she had started to grow up very fast these last few days.

Someone in the crowd muttered: 'They ought to be done for pimping.'

Everybody heard. Sybil Day began to cry and her husband called in his big, decent voice, 'That's a monstrous comment. Come here and say that.'

Iles held up two hands. 'We really don't want intemperate language, ladies and gentlemen, do we? This is a happy occasion. Please. I know some of you feel disappointed at being excluded from details of the story, but you must try to live with it, I'm afraid. I'm sure the Chief Constable will not wish to proceed with this conference if there are any further unpleasantnesses. In this kind of extremely sensitive case it's crucial we all remain balanced and restrained. After all, it is the loss of those qualities which explains these dreadful crimes.'

Harpur thought the conference should be closed now, anyway. They had the girl back, but that was only half the matter. The Lolita Man was still on the loose and probably not far away. There were other kids about. Frustration might be gnawing at him. Would he take a girl to replace the one lost? The sexologists might be able to say what the likelihood of that was, but they didn't carry the can if a child went.

The local *Times* man said: 'Chief, we're not clear how Cheryl-Ann was found. We had a rumour early on that it was as a result of Mr Iles's operation at the Floss. I understand now, though, that the girl was found wandering by two Traffic officers not far from the Pavilions and they informed the Incident Room, where Mr Iles just happened to be. Apparently the Lolita Man was holding her somewhere in the Pavilions and was disturbed this morning by a police search. She took the chance to make a break. Can you put us right on this? We knew about the Floss search, but were you doing the Pavilions as well?'

'We know of no police operation at the Pavilions,' Barton replied.

'Does it matter?' Iles asked. 'Cheryl-Ann is with us. That, surely, is what counts.'

The conference broke up.

Iles cornered Harpur. 'It was you, was it, up at those fucking Pavilions this morning? Where did you get your information from? You've been sitting on something, you sod. You let me work my balls off up at the Floss while you tried to clean up. I'm going to look damn hard into this. Don't think you'll win any *gloire* out of it. You and Garland, a slimy little team, go your own way regardless of the general need, holding hands with the Papes, I wouldn't be surprised.' He seemed to change tone, in the sudden way only Iles could. 'Listen – Garland and my wife: don't think I'm prejudiced against him because of that. I hope I can keep personal matters out of my work. I know there are some men who have to take whatever they can get. We're chasing one now. But I'll admit that business with Sarah doesn't make Garland my favourite son. What the hell does she see in him, the jumped-up jerk?'

'Perhaps she likes jumped-up jerks, sir.'

'A fair point.'

'Garland's at the Pavilions now, seeing if he can get anything more on the Lolita Man – maybe his new vehicle.'

'Harpur, in a couple of minutes we'll see this girl and I'll talk td her and bring the whole story out in no time. I shan't want you sticking your oar in, nor that money-grubbing pair, her parents. My God, what a turn-round. One day they're prostrate with anxiety, the next they sign on the dotted line for the *Daily Armpit*. This interview with the girl requires some handling: determined but delicate. You'd be nowhere. You've got the delicacy, but that's all. A couple of words from this kid and the Lolita Man is ours, so I shan't want anyone to mess it up. And that goes for him, too.' He nodded towards Barton. 'Jolly Ced.'

The Days and Barton approached. 'A distasteful couple of minutes, Desmond,' the Chief said.

'Eric, Sybil, it was intolerable,' Iles replied. 'I feel in a way responsible for allowing such enormities to occur, for permitting foul insults to be levelled in that fashion. These appalling people think of nothing but their own narrow interests. They certainly had decent feelings once, but put them in a weighted bag and dropped it in the river. It's a joining ritual supervised by the NUJ.'

'Must you question her so soon?' Sybil asked. 'Doctors, now this.'

'Darling, they have to,' Day told her. 'The man is free. We all know he could do it again.'

'I'll handle it myself, Sybil,' Iles said. 'It will be done with absolute tact and gentleness.'

Barton looked startled. 'Colin had better go with you. I think he has met this child socially. It will help.'

'Certainly, sir,' Iles replied. 'I was going to suggest that, in fact.'

He and Harpur left the bar with the Days and crossed the road to the hospital. In the corridor outside Cheryl-Ann's room a couple of reporters waited on tubular chairs, guarding their paper's purchase.

One of them said, 'We'd like to sit in on your interview, if that's all right. We wouldn't say anything, of course.'

'Get lost,' Harpur told them.

'Look here, we've paid a lot of money for this. Why not ask Mr and Mrs Day what they think?'

'I couldn't care less what they think.'

'We'll take this up with Barton.'

'You'll find him a charmer.'

Iles put an arm around each of them. Who knew when you might need friends in the Press? 'Boys, you'll get your chance, in due course. I'll see to that, personally. But this is Mr Harpur's case. I can't overrule him, I fear.'

Cheryl-Ann was lying propped up, looking very white and very thin, eyes open, apparently quite alert. Harpur found it difficult to imagine now how she could have struck a sexual chord in him. Her face at least looked unmarked. She had been eating pink ice-cream and there were smears of it on her chin. Sybil wiped them off with a tissue and tutted and clucked. The child was a child again.

Her parents sat on one side of the bed, Iles and Harpur on the other.

'Here's Mr Harpur, darling,' Sybil said. 'You remember him. You met his daughters.'

Harpur recalled the diary entry for that day. 'Their father is police. He began asking questions I didn't like.' He might not ask any at all today.

'And Mr Iles, too. You saw him this morning.'

Iles said softly: 'Hello, Cheryl-Ann. You're looking much better already.'

'It's because I'm thinking about the money for my story.'

'What will you buy?'

'Something serious.'

'Serious?'

'Not kids' things. Investments?'

Iles smiled: 'Good. You seem to have become a very mature young lady. I think you'll want to help us. We'd like you to tell us a bit of your story – even though we're not paying!'

'Which bit?' She sounded worried and tired, as if she knew well enough which bit and was not sure she wanted to talk about it.

'Well, we want to hear about the man. We have to find him quickly.'

There were rope marks on her wrists, as on those early two victims, and perhaps on her ankles, under the sheet, too.

'Some other questions can come later, when you're quite well,' Iles said. 'Now, if you can just help us locate this man who – who hurt you.'

'Yes, he did, he did.' She closed her eyes and turned her head away on the pillow. Tears forced their way from under the lids and spread on her pale cheeks, though she made no sound.

'Don't think about it now, darling,' Sybil told her. 'Just tell these officers where they can find the man and then you can have a sleep.'

'You were up at the Pavilions?' Iles asked.

'Yes, now and then. He had a hut there, but it's not his real place. I never went there. Sometimes I was in the hut, sometimes just in the car. He used to lock me in the boot.' She cried again.

'Well, we'll find that chalet and talk to the people nearby about him. First, though, we'd better know what you called him. What's his name?'

'He never told me.'

'How did you talk to him? Did you talk?'

'I'd call him Dark Eyes.'

'That's a strange name. We heard it from your call to Hazel. Did he tell you to call him that?'

She nodded.

'And does that mean he had dark eyes?'

'Yes.'

'We thought so.' Iles produced some pictures of the dummy. 'Is this what he looked like, Cheryl-Ann?'

She took the photographs and glanced at them, then shook her head slowly. 'This man is dead, isn't he?'

'But was he something like that?'

'This one reminds me of a model in a shop window.'

'But he has dark eyes.'

'They're dead eyes,' she insisted wearily.

Although he had hurt her, she could not bear to think of him like that. To Harpur there seemed to be a battle going on inside the girl. She thought she should be grown-up now, what she called serious, but there was something still there of the romancing child, the child who longed to believe all was wonderful, and whose imagination would make it wonderful.

'All right, Cheryl-Ann,' Iles said. 'You have no name for him. Tell us everything you noticed. I'm sure you are very observant. Does he talk like the people around here?'

'No, he's only here now and then.'

'Where else does he go?'

'Mozambique.'

'Why Mozambique?'

'His property.'

'You're sure about this?'

'That's what he said. He's abroad often.'

The dreamer in her seemed to have won. Weren't her dreams better than the truths she had found? Mr Dark Eyes from Mozambique and Peru and St Trope and Malaga had turned out to be a buggering rapist who kept her tied in a shack or in the boot of a rattling Merc. Was Cheryl-Ann going to admit that to police, or anyone else? Once in a while she might try to sound grown-up and to look at things as they really were. But she was safe now and could retreat into her imagination as soon as the dark pressures came. Jesus, why not? It could be an instinctive bit of self-preservation: if she thought and spoke about what had really happened, and who he really was, her mind would not be able to take the memory of it and might cave in.

Those reporters were going to get something good for their £30,000. It wouldn't be completely true, but it would be glossy. She yearned to tell it. This would be better than a secret diary. She would have a readership, plus the funds. Of course, the reporters wouldn't believe all she said. They would have to take what she gave, though, and so would Iles.

'If he works in Mozambique he'll be easy to trace,' the ACC said.

'Not works. Property – his investments,' she corrected, very patiently.

Sybil took her daughter's hand. 'I wonder if you're all right, darling. Should we stop now, Desmond? Might she be rambling a little?'

'Soon,' he said. 'We must know whether he has a different car now. Did he steal something else after the old blue Mercedes, Cheryl-Ann?'

'His car was blue, but not an old Mercedes.'

'I see,' Iles replied. 'What car did he have?'

Harpur could have answered for her.

'A blue Lagonda.'

'A Lagonda?'

'She knows about cars,' Day said.

Sybil looked embarrassed: 'I'm sorry, Desmond.'

Iles spoke more quietly, perhaps in an attempt to soften what he was going to say, perhaps because of the reporters outside. 'Listen, Cheryl-Ann, you're not really helping us, are you? I thought you'd become very sensible and mature, but all this sounds like children's stuff, now doesn't it?' He laughed grandly, inviting her to agree that she had been spinning an amusing, mischievous yarn.

She did not laugh in response. 'I've told you what I know.'

Iles grew grave, and his voice hardened. 'You're giving us eyewash. This man has insulted your body, love, violated you, bound you, imprisoned you, and yet it sounds as if you don't want us to catch him. All right, you've taken a shine to him. That can happen, we know. But you understand he would have killed you, don't you?'

Day stood up in protest. 'No, this really can't go on. You are making her relive the whole terrible thing.'

'Would you mind being silent? I want some fragments of truth out of your daughter, not the undiscovered works of Berta Ruck. Can't you realise, Cheryl-Ann, that this man might kill another child if we don't get him? You were very lucky. Five other girls weren't. Do you really want us to waste time looking for a Lagonda when you know he drives something else, may be using it to snatch a girl while we speak?'

'Now, this is enough,' Sybil said. Cheryl-Ann had sunk down in the bed and pulled the sheet over her head.

Iles looked at her. 'Yes, I suppose you could be right. There may still be a degree of shock present. It's natural enough. I hear they're going to discharge her tomorrow. We'll talk again, perhaps, when she's at home, in her own surroundings.'

'Indeed, yes,' Day said.

The two journalists were still at their posts in the corridor, but made no attempt to speak this time.

'I believe that tough little creature is trying to shield him,' Iles told Harpur.

'Or herself.'

'What the hell does that mean?'

'That she's not so tough. She needs a screen between now and then.'

'Oh, you're speaking as a psychologist, are you? I'd forgotten that was one of your specialisations. I notice you asked not one question in there – a smirking, superior silence.'

'You told me to keep out of it, sir.'

'Granted. In matters of extreme delicacy, such as the mental balance of a child, it would obviously be inhuman for more than one questioner to be engaged. That's all I meant, Col. It wouldn't have mattered which of us interviewed the poor child. Lying little wretch filled me up with all sorts of purple rot. Property in Mozambique. Jesus, I could have strangled her, and her bloody smarmy, grasping parents. Mind you, they have been through hell, one has to remember that and make adequate allowance. It's so splendid to be involved even in the smallest way in restoring their child to them, in bringing back some happiness to their lives. God knows, it's a role we are able to play all too infrequently, particularly in this appalling case. All the cash to go to the kid, my arse. That dignitary, Eric, will just have to exercise a guiding hand over all those fat noughts, won't he? I'd bet he gets more than a couple of thermal vests out of it.'

25

She has gone. On the radio they said she escaped. It isn't true. I let her go. She wasn't like the others. I don't know what made her different, maybe because she didn't seem so afraid, maybe because she had that terrible fight with me in the telephone box, I didn't know she could be so strong. Some of that swearing and being so strong seemed to make her not like a young girl then but like some hard old cow. I didn't want to keep her for ever after that. She knew all sorts of the worst words, not just damn and arse, although the school she goes to is supposed to be good. I don't want to think now of the words she used or I'll never be able to sleep, I'll be sick, but they were not words I would expect from a young girl who wears a straw hat.

She can tell them about me now, I know that. But she doesn't know my real place, only that old place I used to live in so long ago at the Pavilions where we went now and then. People were rushing all over the place up there because the police came and I just let her go, that was all.

I had her eyes covered when we were in the new car after the Merc but she might be able to tell something about it. She didn't see it, but she was in it and she might be able to tell them about what size it is and things like that, she's bright.

It said on the radio that the big ape, Harpur, was going to see her in the hospital and someone else with him. She'll tell them everything, of course she will. I don't know why she's in hospital, she wasn't sick, she could swear and fight all right, and rip my medallion away, I'll never be lucky again.

I don't care now. It's all coming to an end for me, I think. All I want is a good sleep. It really upset me when she did all that filthy screaming and swearing, a girl like that, it made me think there are no really clean, sweet girls, left, even when they are so young. It was a bad time for me when I thought that for the first time. There doesn't seem anything left in life.

God, I am feeling bad tonight, now she is gone. Maybe I

shouldn't feel so sad about it, maybe it's not so bad. All girls might not be like her. I have met nicer ones, ones I didn't want to let go, ever, because they were right for me. Maybe I could still find another girl like that. It would have to be very soon, because I feel so bad and so much in despair. I need a girl who would show me soon that things are not all dirty and violent and spoiled. I might be able to feel better if I could find a girl who would show me that again. Perhaps there'll be no time to watch and choose, like before. I don't think that matters. I did watch a long time last time and I thought this was the right girl, but it was a girl who cursed so badly, like a fucking soldier.

There was another girl I noticed sometimes in that school. They cannot all be like this last one, they can't. This other girl was younger, and that's good. She might not have had time to learn all the filth and violence. This is why the young girls are best.

26

Harpur began his walks once more. He felt sure that the Lolita Man would either act again soon, or get out of the area, afraid he would be found. He could not know how little reliable information Cheryl-Ann provided.

Harpur found himself tempted to go back and watch Ash Tree, but suspected this was only because it lay near Ruth's house. Surely, the Lolita Man would stay away from there now, knowing the attention that police would give the school. Instead, Harpur toured parks and youth clubs again and some of the comprehensives. Occasionally he watched John Locke itself and saw his daughters leaving for home, though they did their best to ignore him: it hurt their status to be daughters of a cop and they always tried to play it down.

One afternoon, while Harpur was not present, the Days brought Cheryl-Ann to the house again to see Hazel and Jill. Megan had asked him to stay away.

'They want to reintroduce her gradually to ordinary life and children of her own age,' she said. 'It makes sense. She's not going back to school this term, of course. It's difficult after all that terrible stuff in the papers.'

'We'd have to put a guard on her if she did go back.'

'That brings me to something a bit sensitive, darling,' she had said. 'Sybil doesn't want to be misunderstood, but she thinks it would be better if you weren't here when they bring Cheryl-Ann. Sybil's still rather apprehensive about all that.'

'All what?'

'You know, don't you, Colin? Police. Questioning and so on. It's to be expected.'

'Sure. They just wanted us to get the kid back, and then we become a pain.'

'Oh, please, Col, not your Kipling turn.'

'Which is that?'

> *'It's Tommy this, an' Tommy that, an' "Chuck him out the brute!"*
> *But it's "Saviour of 'is country" when the guns begin to shoot.*

For "thin red line" read "thin blue line".'

'It's an education living here.'

He made sure he was walking on the afternoon the Days came. Jill told him afterwards that Cheryl-Ann talked mainly about what she would do with the money from the paper.

'Could she be diseased after contact with that man?' Hazel asked.

'She's been seen by doctors,' he replied. 'Do you think that you two worry over-much about hygiene?'

'Oh, we know that rigmarole about all the best people having it – Mozart et cetera. We're not in that class.'

Then, the day after Cheryl-Ann's visit, in the last week of Ash Tree School's term, a girl one form down from hers disappeared on the way home. Nobody saw anything and the parents, who both worked, did not realise what had happened until they arrived at their house three hours after school closed for the day. Harpur went out there with Garland, and Iles brought his blackboard back into the Incident Room.

'We can't be sure, can we, that it's this Lolita Man again?' the wife asked. About thirty-five, short and dark, she was doing better at holding herself together than her husband.

'Of course not,' Garland said.

'Children wander,' Harpur added. 'Girls of this age, especially. I've got a couple myself.'

'She doesn't wander,' the man said. 'Nothing like this has ever happened before.'

'She's getting a little older all the time,' Garland said.

'But from the same school!' the wife exclaimed. 'Surely it should have been watched.'

Surely it should have been.

'He obviously knew that territory,' the woman went on. 'He might have spotted Sîan while he was watching the other girl. Shouldn't the police have considered that possibility?'

Yes, they should have.

Garland said: 'We've got a huge area to cover. We're trying to read a sick mind, but one that has always behaved to some pattern previously. There were good distances between his other attacks, two not even on our ground, you see.'

'Would she go with a man who offered a lift?' Harpur asked.

'She's been told not to,' the man said. 'Who knows, though?' Possibly a little younger than his wife, he sat hunched, a tall, lean, balding man, his face very white now. Without looking up he asked: 'Is it true we have seventy-two hours? That's what the papers say.'

'They'd say anything,' Garland replied.

'But there is a pattern?' the man said. 'You just told us that.'

'I was talking about distances.'

'Isn't there a police blackboard with the hours left on it?' he asked. 'Several papers said so.'

'Nothing of the sort,' Harpur replied. 'They got that from some American film.'

The wife said, 'How is it that this last girl wasn't –? How is it that she came back? Did he let her go?'

'She says she escaped,' her husband answered. 'It's in the papers.'

'He may have let her go. He might be changing,' Harpur said.

'So it's not hopeless?' the wife asked. She answered herself.

'No, of course not. We're talking as if it has to be this same man. The little madam could roll up here any time, saying she's been to the pictures or . . . or something.' She tailed off, as if suspecting that none of them believed her.

'Exactly,' Garland said. 'And even if it is the Lolita Man, we've been very close to him, we think. He's making mistakes all the time.'

'We made a mistake letting her come home from school alone,' the man said.

'No, you mustn't blame yourself,' Harpur told them. 'Logic said it would not happen at the same place twice.'

'Whose logic?'

'We think something is happening to the –' Harpur had been going to say that the Lolita Man's mind might be breaking up. What sort of comfort would that be, though, to parents of a child in his hands? 'We think the Lolita Man is losing his touch. We believe his return to the school – if it really is our man – could be one of his biggest mistakes yet.'

'Why?' the man asked.

Harpur said: 'Is your daughter keen on writing things down? Might there be any letters, a diary? Could we have a look around?'

Once again he found himself turning over a child's possessions and clothes and once again he felt like a thick-fingered heavy. The parents watched. 'Sîan would be very young to keep a diary,' the mother said. 'Very young for – Well, just very young.'

When they returned to the Incident Room, Barton was once more in front of the big map and once more seemingly dazed by the problems it offered. Harpur could sympathise. 'This is like something Scriptural, Colin: a curse on us – impossible to fight or beat. The thing mocks us.' Going closer to the map he studied a green dot, signifying a road-block, as if he wished to be part of it, wished physically to help them check and search. 'We've got a bloody team here from the Home Office, did you know? It's because of all that vile press stuff about non-cooperation with Ethan. Christ, can I do without that now! This is a Deputy Under-Secretary, a couple of Under-Secretaries from the Police Department, and God knows who else. We're going to get screwed by an army of Homos. They've already said we're to hold joint briefings for all senior officers working on the case, starting at once. The only consolation is that they'll piss on next door as well. I don't see Ethan making the Inspectorate after this.'

There was the kind of sudden stir in the room that signalled some black, new development and a sergeant brought a message sheet hurriedly to Barton. In a while he said: 'A girl's body has been found at the old aerodrome. She's about twelve. It seems to fit. She's received what looks like the standard sexual attention, probably not too competent, but he tried. First indications are that she has been strangled manually. That's the pattern, isn't it? It's probably my turn to break it to the parents, I think.'

'Mr Iles prides himself on handling that sort of thing, sir.'

'Yes, Desmond has a range of genuine abilities. Don't be wholly put off by the bursts of egomania.'

Harpur drove out alone to the old aerodrome. It was a routine: the detective saw the body because the body and the site might give him leads. But these visits to the dead had come to seem typical of something hopeless and end-stopped in the case. He wanted to be driving towards the man who had done this, yet knew he would probably see nothing today that would suddenly give the search direction. Barton was not so far out: a curse on the land.

Uniformed men under an inspector were taping off the area when he arrived. The body lay still uncovered against a wall of what had once been the Customs office, now roofless and windowless and invaded by weeds and grass. A sheep ran out as Harpur drew up.

'The doctor's on his way, sir, and Mr Iles, I believe,' the inspector said.

It was like a replay of the King Richard, a deadly, unpreventable cycle. He bent to look at the girl – another distorted, young face, another protruding tongue. 'Have you found the clothes?'

'Yes, sir, most of them, I think. Inside the building or near. This whole bloody place should have been cleared and developed years ago. We're organising a proper search over the full area.'

'Identification?'

'Yes. Name-tags in some garments.'

Who would come and look and say the final yes or no? The father usually did that job, but this one might not be up to it.

Iles arrived with a man of about forty in a Norfolk jacket and walking boots. 'Colin, this is Mr Shebbear – or Jake, if I may – of the Home Office party. He asked if he might come out with me. Luckily he was equipped for field work. This is Colin Harpur, head of CID, in charge of the cases.' Iles walked over to the body, Shebbear following. 'Little one, little one,' Iles grieved, 'why did they let you out alone? Just a baby. Milk teeth.'

'She'd be about twelve, I suppose,' Shebbear said.

'I'm glad you're here, Jake. It will be a help,' Iles replied. He bent, as Harpur had before. 'Those eyes, my God, look at them – they're still used to kids' TV and comic books, and think what they've seen out here.'

Shebbear moved off to inspect some of the buildings.

'A prick,' Iles reported, 'but no more than one would have expected, Col. I can understand why they're here, understand entirely. There is great disquiet, and reasonable disquiet, that we get no nearer this strange lover. Any Government would have to look into allegations that police rivalries are leading to deaths of this sort. Well, we'll give these fuckers – Jake, and the Deputy Under-sodding-Secretary and the Assistant Under-sodding-Secretary *et al* a good run for their money. The Deputy Under-Secretary himself is very fine. Several Blues, at least.'

Shebbear called something and Iles moved nearer to hear him better, then nodded. He came back to Harpur. 'Jake thinks the man probably knew the area well, since this aerodrome is an ideal site for such a crime.'

'Someone might have seen a vehicle,' Harpur said.

'People come out to give their kids a lesson in the family car,' the inspector told them. 'And there's some amateur stock-carring. I'm afraid another vehicle might not be noticed.'

Iles drew Harpur away. 'Jake and his chums have been looking for material we failed to pass on to the Incense Burners,

Col. They hit on four descriptions of a man spotted around the Canberra Avenue area by an old cow busybody and once actually glimpsed naked at an upstairs window in a state of semi-arousal and eyeing schoolgirls on their way home. A big, menacing type of man, apparently.'

'I see.'

'Reasonably enough, I thought, the Homos asked why these details had not been transmitted to the county. I could hardly say it was our Detective Chief Super making welfare visits to a former colleague's widow.'

'No. What did you say?'

'Oh, that we'd checked the man out and he was just a harmless old flasher and wanker.'

'Thanks.'

'It's the team thing, Col. Stick together.'

'I'll remember.'

More police and experts were assembling around the girl. Shebbear returned. 'This is extremely difficult ground to search, what with debris and so on. It will have to be done, though, in case the child resisted and something was torn from him, a button, say. Look, I do hope you don't feel I'm teaching my grandmother how to suck eggs.'

'My grandmother used to get in a God-awful mess whenever she tried it,' Iles replied. 'Yolk from flat hat to black boots.'

They were photographing the body. Iles went and picked up a tarpaulin, ready to cover the child as soon as the work was finished.

'I've a feeling you know a lot more about this than you let on,' Shebbear told Harpur.

'Bugger all. I know she's dead and I hope I know who she is. What I don't know is who *he* is.'

Megan was away for the day again so Harpur went home briefly to make sure the girls had come in from school and check where they were going for the evening. This case had really begun to get to him. He and Jill did the evening meal, according to rota.

Hazel asked: 'What happened about that girl's book, dad?'

'The diary? I put it back.'

'After you'd read it.'

'You didn't mention it to her, I hope. She'd be hurt.'

'You told me not to tell anybody.'

'I tell you not to do all sorts of things. It makes no difference.'

'It was clever to put it back.'

'Oh?'

'Does she still write in it?'

'How do I know?'

'Why did you put it back, then?'

'It's hers, that's all.'

'Shouldn't you look and see whether she's put anything in it since she came back? Aren't you supposed to be some sort of detective? No wonder they send action men down from London. That's what the papers say.'

'The diary was all rubbishy, dad, wasn't it?' Jill said.

'Very.'

Yes, rubbishy, but what else did he have? In the night he left the Incident Room and, thinking about what Hazel had said, made his way to the Days' house once more, taking the half-mile on foot, as before. This time there were no lights in the house: the Days could sleep again. He went swiftly to the changing hut at the side of the pool and once inside switched on his flashlight. The Dolfino box was where he had left it on the shelf near the window, and taking it down he found the diary still under the mask. Perhaps she had lost interest in it now, forgotten about it. He sat on the floor and turned immediately to the end of the diary. At once he saw that Hazel was right. Cheryl-Ann had been writing since her return. When he examined the diary earlier it had finished with a note for 30 June, the day before she went. Now, there were several completed pages after this. He read the first of them, dated 7 July, and found the clash of dreams and reality in front of him once more.

This was the diary of a child before this, but many events have occurred which make all that earlier part seem very childish. I have come home and it is so wonderful and safe here. When I was like I was before I thought he was wonderful. I've read that just now, but he was just mad and cruel and dirty, even if he did not kill me.

Others I still tell parts of the lies I used to write before because I would still like to believe they were true, though I know they're not. I tell this to the police and the journalists. I don't want them to know I was taken away in a terrible old Mercedes, with rust and so noisy. Sometimes I don't want to think of it like that myself, even. I told them all the childish things about a Lagonda and Mozambique. They didn't believe it. The reporters did not put that in the paper. They put that old Merc in the paper because the police knew about that when it was found and they said he probably works abroad, not Mozambique or investments. They are too crafty. Being grown-up they seem to know what is real. They only believe some of the things I say. But they paid the money.

Harpur switched off the flashlight, got up from the floor, opened the door of the shed quietly and listened. He thought he had heard a sound from somewhere in the house, but although he waited several minutes there was no repetition and the windows remained dark.

Returning to his spot, he put on the flashlight again and turned to the next diary page. 'All rubbishy,' Jill had said, and he was beginning to get the feeling that had come to him when reading her notes before: a sense of drowning in wool and froth, even if it was a different kind of wool and froth now.

8 July
They all call him the Lolita Man in the papers, which is to do with a film, but they have not got it in the video shop, I tried today. Also, it is a book and I may be able to get this in the library, I did not see a paperback of it in the newspaper shop. It's a book about a man who falls in love with a girl who is young and goes away with her, a nurse in the hospital told me. The girl does not mind, he is nice to her. This is not like what happened to me, I can't write it.

The nurse said he couldn't stand grown-up women and he used to laugh at the girl's mother when she wasn't looking because she was thirty-six, which some would not consider old. But this one I was with he had also been with grown-up women and he said this when he lost his medallion that time near the telephone box, when I tried to telephone home and we were fighting. After, he was screaming that medallion was luck and it was given to him by a woman who bought it and she knew the real place he lived because he took her there once.

Then he became so cruel and he said it was because I had been swearing when we were fighting. I only called him a fuck-pig and a shit-heap, which is not big deal. We often call the teachers this. But what he was really angry about was this medallion and the woman called Debbie. He tried to make me jealous and he was talking about her all the time, with red leather trousers and her own flat, I didn't care. If she went with him she must be a fuck-pig and a shit-heap.

9 July

I can tell that lots of people are really very curious to find out what happened when I was away with him, they say to me did he treat you well, that is their way of asking what he did, because they don't want to say it straight out, it would look as if they might be dirty-minded. There is a policeman called Iles, he asks straight out, but they are hearing these things all the time, it doesn't interest them. He has been to the house yesterday and the day before and I like him. He's a bit mad and also kind, not like other police. He gets ratty, but I don't mind, I like watching his face go all colours, and then he gets kind again, he seems to have read everything in the world. I don't tell him anything that is true and he knows this and it makes him angry but not for very long. Now and then I see him turn his head and he's muttering big swear words to himself about me, not just fuck-pig and shit-heap, but really deep ones, what they call export only at school. He makes me laugh. I . . .

Behind Harpur the door opened quietly and he turned, swinging the flashlight beam and standing up. 'Hello, Cheryl-Ann,' he said.

'My name's Jennifer.' She was in blue cotton pyjamas, a pair he had handled twice in her room. Her feet were bare. 'Who are you?' she asked.

He took the light off her face and shone it on his own. 'Oh, police again.'

'Were you coming to do some writing?'

'Uh?'

'In the diary.'

'It's the middle of the night. I saw a light.'

'Did you wake up your parents?'

'Uh? Why should I?'

'Who did you think it was?'

'I didn't know, did I? That's why I came to see. Can I have my book, please? It's no good now, if someone has seen it. Did you see it before? Of course you did. When I came back I thought it was not in exactly the right place. I should have thought of that. I suppose you were too grown-up and clever to go looking for all those cars. I was just a crazy kid in those days, you know.'

She looked more childlike than ever tonight, thin and still pale, bony, awkward, very fragile.

'Have you got what's called one of those shredders down at your nick?' she asked.

'Of course.'

She handed back the diary. 'Get rid of it.'

'Did you tell him about the diary?'

She seemed to consider this for a time. 'Now and then, when people ask you one thing they're really asking you something else, aren't they?'

'Sometimes. Why do you say that, though?'

She smiled slightly. 'I think you want to know did I think it was him here now when I came down from my bed, not telling anyone. You think I really would like to go back to him, don't you?'

'No. I didn't mean that.'

She smiled again. 'People are very funny.' She frowned. 'His breath. Filthy. All that smoking, and bad teeth, I think. This was because he was abroad so often, in places such as Moz – oh, shit, I'm starting all that again.'

'You ought to go back to bed now.' He felt like a father addressing a child and regarded this as a very big improvement in himself. Perhaps he had grown up a bit, too.

'You should be careful, you know,' she said. 'There are police about here all the time now. It's because I could be what's called a target.'

'I know. Luckily, I'm informed about where they patrol.'

'Anyway, while you're all watching me, he takes another girl.'

'Yes.'

She turned and began walking across the garden back to the house but she seemed to shiver and hugged herself.

'Don't hang about,' he said. 'You'll be weak, still.'

'I'm rich, you know.'

He would have liked to go back home and make sure Megan had returned and the girls were all right, but instead drove at once into Ethan land to call on Debbie and Robert again. It was after 3 a.m. when he arrived, poor sods. The door had been patched up, though with the old lock still in place: there were better things to spend Lane's tenner on than Mr Yale. Harpur knocked this time and kept knocking, no longer having to worry about a hostage. He liked to think of himself as a kid-glove cop, even if the bourgeoisie up the Days' way did regard him as thuggish. When all this was over he'd find out who said that and get some Traffic boys to have a look at their tyres.

There was movement inside. 'Is that you police buggers again?' Robert shouted. No lights came on and the door stayed shut.

Harpur called back: 'This is only a courtesy call. Can you open up or shall we just come in, anyway?'

'I been to a solicitor.'

Harpur gave the door a moderate kick.

'All right, all right.' In a moment the door opened. 'Where are the rest?' Robert asked.

'Surrounding the place. We heard you had a big team in.'

Debbie appeared in the corridor wearing the dressing gown.

'Just a couple of things I thought of after we left,' Harpur said to her. 'I wonder if I could have two words with you on your own, love.'

'No way,' Robert replied. He had put jeans on before opening the door.

'I'm not going to try anything with her,' Harpur said. 'I'm off it – having a late Lent this year.' He took Robert by the shoulder, shoved him out into the kitchen and shut the door. 'Don't come in, there's a sport.'

He and Debbie sat down in the living room. 'Now, I understand your difficulty the other night. You don't want to offend Rob, or lose him, he's a great fellow. But you knew this lad, Dave, better than you said, didn't you? It wasn't just one night here. You lied to us. That's not good.'

She became angry. 'I never.'

'He took you to his real place. All right, he uses some shack up at the Pavilions now and then, but it's not his proper house.'

'I don't know about that.'

'Debbie, you do.'

'All I know is what he told me.'

'He thought a lot of you. He wanted to show you his real place, didn't he? You were important to him. And he really prized that medallion. He didn't steal it, did he? You gave it to him. No wonder you never claimed.'

She put a hand to her face and fingered her skin agitatedly. 'Have you found him, then?'

'Not yet.'

'Who told you all this – all this rubbish?'

'It's right, isn't it?'

For a moment she kept silent. 'He was nice, in his funny way. I was by myself. He never touched me, even at his place. I just gave him the phoenix for luck. He needed it.'

'I don't care what happened between you, Debbie. And I'm not going to say anything to Robert. But I've got to know where he lives. He's killed another child and nobody can say now where it will stop. You were very reasonable last time you heard how serious it was, even if you did lie. Well, it's worse now. He's losing control. I've got to have him, tonight.'

She thought. 'I don't know no address. We just went there.'

'Could you take me?'

'What about Rob?'

'He's no part of it. Come on, we go now.'

'I'm not dressed.'

'We'll be back in an hour. He won't know you've been out.'

He was in strange territory, thank the Lord, and not likely to be recognised. What could some ever-open-eye make of seeing him driving at 3.30 a.m. with a scrubber in a dressing gown? Debbie took him to an area of dockland streets, still in Ethan's realm, and they parked near a mouldering, tin-built Seamen's Mission with peeling texts on the façade: 'I am the Way', 'Boast not thyself of tomorrow'. But it was already tomorrow and dawn had begun to show across the dark water. From some shebeen not far away heavy rock still boomed and he heard an occasional shout or laugh behind it: the Seamen's Mission was in a very competitive market and, if it really wanted to be the Way, might need to smarten up. Debbie pointed up a cul-de-sac of tiny, old, stone cottages opening straight on to the street. 'The third.'

Briefly he thought about telephoning Lane. There were all kinds of reasons for informing him: if you went on someone's ground you did that as a courtesy, and he seemed pretty straight. Again, Ethan would tear Lane apart if Harpur made the arrest here this morning. The Home Office gang might not think too much of it, either, if Harpur gave a spectacular demonstration of how to cut the other lot out and make fools of them in their own manor.

In any case, this was not a one-man job. The houses had small back-yards opening on to a lane, with dock buildings behind. If you made a mess of surprising your man in one of these places he could be out and away, front or back, and into a criss-cross of rough streets or a complex of big, shadowy warehouses and works. Even with a dozen men it might not be easy. There would be no aid from local citizenry down here.

He decided against telling Lane, all the same. This could be the end of the whole thing, with Debbie waiting in the car and able to make an identification. It was not that he particularly wanted to keep it from Lane: he wanted to keep it from everybody, until things were parcelled and sealing-waxed. If the Homos didn't like it they could go and jump in the dock. Of course they would like it. All they wanted was the bastard nailed and an end to allegations that law and order had finally gone down the tube.

An H registration Ford Zephyr stood outside the little house. For his vehicles, at least, this lad did like size. Never mind the age, look at the length. Harpur went quickly around to the rear, climbed over a bit of a wall and approached the house through a yard full of junk and scrap. Was the Lolita Man a gypsy? The door felt as if it was on a bolt and did not yield when Harpur pushed. Timber had been timber when this property was built. He turned away and went to work on a window catch with his pocket knife and in a couple of minutes forced the lever back and was able to enter. For a moment he used the flashlight. Everything looked neat and new and comfortable. Perhaps the Lolita Man saved a bit when he was working on the rig, or whatever it might be, and put the cash into his home. After all, you'd need somewhere nice to come back to after strangling a kid.

Quickly he looked around the ground floor and then went upstairs as silently as he could make it. All doors off the minute landing were shut and he stood for a second trying to guess what might be what. He tried one, pushing it open fast as he had been taught, but found a shower room, looking as if it had been put in lately, probably with a grant. Mr Dark Eyes must often have rhapsodised about this gem to colleagues and advisers down in Mozambique and Peru. He was turning out a real *Homes and Gardens* man, except for the garden: never mind, didn't he have use of an empty airfield no distance away?

He tried another door, with the same swift, violent technique, designed to scare rigid anyone inside and give time to get an arm-hold. The curtains had been tightly drawn but he made out a bed, with maybe someone in it. He caught the sharp smell of whisky. 'Dave, Dave, boy. We've found your phoenix for you. Like to rise up now?' he said.

There was no movement. Harpur switched on his flashlight and saw the dark head of a man, the face away from him. A one and a half litre duty-free Johnnie Walker flask containing maybe an inch of Scotch in the bottom stood on a bedside table, and near it a brown, plastic pill bottle lay on its side with the top off, empty.

Harpur put on the bedroom light and went quickly round to the far side of the bed. The dummy had not been a bad likeness, after all, and nobody could have said now which looked deader than the other. That last little girl had failed to bring him comfort, then.

'I'll need help here, I think,' he told Debbie, back at the car. 'I'll take you home first.' It no longer seemed important for her to identify him. Jennifer, who used to be Cheryl-Ann, who used to be Jennifer, would have to do that.

'Is he there?' Debbie asked.

'Yes. You did well.'

'Will he – well, is he going to stay, if you leave?'

'Yes, he will.'

'Did he mention about the medallion? Or anything – our time together?' She sounded wistful. 'I'd like to talk to him again.'

This, Harpur decided to ignore. He said: 'The medallion is definitely coming back to you. Give it to Rob?'

'Maybe.'

'That lad has had a lot to put up with.'

'He's got no charm whatsoever.'

'Charm? Little of that about anywhere, Deb.'

After dropping her he found a telephone and at about 4.30 a.m. called Lane, saying only that he thought he had the Lolita Man's address. What kudos was there in finding a corpse on your own?

'Another one?' Lane mumbled from his bed.

'This could be good.'

'If you say so. After all, we're partners.'

'Right.'

Harpur had carefully relocked the window and they broke in through there together. For the sake of realism, he repeated his original error and threw open the shower room door yelling, 'Police! Keep still.'

'He's in here,' Lane said.

'My God.'

'He had sleeping problems.'

'Over-sensitive, that was his trouble.'

'No bloody note or anything.' Lane was opening drawers. He picked out what looked like some sort of work permit. 'Seems as if he did a bit of free-lance labouring in France.' He went on searching. 'Can we tie him good to all the cases?'

'Does it matter? We've got the Day girl.'

'That's only one. Nice job for a kid.'

'Worse has happened to her.'

'That's what I mean. Does she want to see him again, dead or alive?'

'She believes in facing the real. This is it.'

'I'll get some newspaper cuttings of all the cases and put them in the food cupboard downstairs, as if he'd been making a secret collection,' Lane said. 'Coroners love that sort of thing.'

'Good thinking.'

27

The Deputy Under-Secretary, Dallian, said: 'Gentlemen, this would have been the first joint briefing of senior officers. I'm delighted to say it has become unnecessary owing to developments during the early hours, which you will all have heard about. Had those developments not taken place, I would not be speaking to you now. A mere Civil Servant has no role in a police briefing. One would have simply observed. I make these, as it were, extramural comments here now by special permission of the two Chiefs, Vincent Ethan and Cedric Barton.

'I want only to say that I and my party came here because of press reports that something was amiss in relationships between the two Forces most involved in these terrible cases.' He paused. 'Gentlemen, I think I can say that the manner in which this matter was brought to a conclusion last night demonstrates as nothing else could the kind of cooperation that has, in fact, been exercised throughout. Senior officers, from both Forces, working in concert, discovered this body together. Perhaps it is not quite the end of the affair which we would all have wished for, but thank God it *is* the end – achieved through excellent, inter-Force detective work. And the same kind of work will enable us to prove this was the man we wanted. I look forward now to a combined press statement which will make those damned journalists eat their hats.'

Ethan and Barton spoke briefly about the new bonds that the case had created between the Forces and Barton added that he could now retire with equanimity and satisfaction in his soul. As Harpur was leaving, Ethan took him by the arm: 'Don't think this is the end of things, you sod. You and Lane, is it? A fine bloody alliance. And you poncing about on my ground. I've got it noted.'

Outside, while Barton and Ethan addressed the Press, Iles said to Harpur: 'Congrats, Col. Some quite astonishing pieces of instinctual – indeed, inspirational – detection, if I may say so. Beautiful. OK, so you've turned Mick-lover. That's your funeral, isn't it? OK, so you've probably let Lane in after Old Mortality. But if that's your idea of positive, decent, loyal behaviour, so be it. I couldn't live with that sort of thing myself, but your sensibilities have been pretty effectively coarsened and stupefied over the years, haven't they?'

That night, as a celebration, Harpur went to see Ruth. After he had been there for an hour there was a knock at the door and she got up, dressed and went to answer. 'It's a cop,' she said, on return.

Jesus. Harpur dressed and went down. 'What? There are kids here, you know. You could wake them.'

'Sorry, sir. We had a call from the lady opposite saying that a suspicious man seen and reported previously was back near their house and she feared he might expose himself at the window. Mr Iles thought it should be checked out.'